D0891769

Grieving for Guava

Grieving for Guava

Stories

Cecilia M. Fernandez

UNIVERSITY PRESS OF KENTUCKY

Scholarly publisher for the Commonwealth,
serving Bellarmine University, Berea College, Centre
College of Kentucky, Eastern Kentucky University,
The Filson Historical Society, Georgetown College,
Kentucky Historical Society, Kentucky State University,
Morehead State University, Murray State University,
Northern Kentucky University, Transylvania University,
University of Kentucky, University of Louisville,
and Western Kentucky University.
All rights reserved.

Editorial and Sales Offices: The University Press of Kentucky
663 South Limestone Street, Lexington, Kentucky 40508-4008
www.kentuckypress.com

Library of Congress Cataloging-in-Publication Data

Names: Fernandez, Cecilia M., 1954– author.
Title: Grieving for guava : stories / Cecilia M. Fernandez.
Description: Lexington, Kentucky : University Press of Kentucky,
    [2020] | Series: The University Press of Kentucky new poetry & prose
    series
Identifiers: LCCN 2019057961 | ISBN 9780813178974 (hardcover ; alk.
    paper) | ISBN 9780813178981 (pdf) | ISBN 9780813178998 (epub)
Subjects: LCSH: Cuba—Emigration and immigration—Fiction. | United
    States—Emigration and immigration—Fiction.
Classification: LCC PS3606.E73344 A6 2020 | DDC 813/.6—dc23
LC record available at https://lccn.loc.gov/2019057961

Member of the Association
of University Presses

For my mother, Cecilia,
who inhabited the world of this book with me,
and for my children,
Alexandra, Andrew, and Christopher,
who led me—not gently—into another

 # Contents

About This Book

Nothing reminds me of my parents' lost island like the smell of guava. Once, at the grocery store, I came across the aromatic fruit of my childhood. I scooped up the leathery brown-gray ball with its hidden fleshy red interior and pressed it to my baby daughter's nose.

"This," I cried, "is what Cuba smells like!"

It is this nostalgia for a land I knew only briefly that afflicts me and many of my friends, the children of the first immigrants who fled from the communist Castro regime that took over in 1959. Nostalgia, the desire for the irrecoverable, springs up at the slightest provocation.

The stories in this book revolve around the fractured lives of Cuban immigrants who privately—and, in many cases, vociferously—grieve for the elusive guava. Friedrich Hegel, in his *Introductory Lectures on Aesthetics,* says: "The world of inwardness celebrates its triumph over the outer world." The sickly inner yearning, certifying the wonders of a lost land, stands in its place. Today the powerful feeling of loss has even gripped the imaginations of the pioneer immigrants' grandchildren who have never seen the island.

As wave upon wave of Cuban immigrants continues to settle in the bustling metropolis of Miami, the city has become indistinguishable from other Latin American capitals. Many of the newcomers don't remember those first immigrants, the trailblazers who set in motion the melding of English and Spanish cultures in South Florida.

The narrator of Lawrence Durrell's novel *Clea* defines his motivation for telling the story of Alexandria, Egypt, a multicultural seaside city not unlike Miami: "to store, to codify, to annotate the past before it was utterly lost." This book is my own small effort to do the same.

Grieving for Guava

Marusa's Beach

Each evening at sundown the three Marusas, mother, daughter, and grandmother, stared out to sea, waves lapping at their feet, hypnotized, until the lights of ships dotted the darkness. The eldest of the trio insisted that beyond the ships, maybe at the edge of madness, she could see the glow of the streetlamps of the Malecón boardwalk, which some said was only ninety miles away.

"La Habana," I heard the grandmother, Marusa I, exclaim one night, "our home!"

"We were happy then," Marusa II moaned into the wind.

"Ahh . . . ahh." This was Marusa III, shaking in her wheelchair. Mouth open, twisted to the side, saliva streaming, right hand curled up tight against her chest not unlike a praying mantis, she screamed until mother and grandmother turned to cross the street back to the old hotel where they lived.

"Está bien, está bien," Marusa II murmured. Abstracted, with an air of desolation, she settled her daughter in the wheelchair and struggled to push it through the sand, stopping once to stroke the girl's thick black hair, upright on her skull. Marusa III shifted to look at her grandmother—graying hair with a bit of a paunch and a hint of a limp—and met the older woman's sad brown eyes with her own bewildered sapphire-blue ones, pupils a pinprick.

Hidden behind a sand dune, I saw Marusa III, twelve years old, close to my age, afflicted with cerebral palsy, a disease I didn't know back then, weeping, choking, gasping for breath with a heaving chest I thought would kill her, something like the epilepsy attack I had witnessed the other day in a boy in class. Looking out to sea crazed her with a desire not hers.

"Hi, Marusa, how are you?" I said when I saw her the next morning.

"Eeee, ahahah," Marusa III answered. I listened to the tone, not the vowels or consonants, and understood. She sat in the wheelchair, her grandmother next to her on the wide veranda with peeling paint that separated our hotel from the street. Beyond spread the mighty killer ocean, all the way out to the horizon where we could see freighters steaming out of the Port of Miami day and night. I talked to Marusa about school, my dog in Cuba, my books; she nodded, smiling, rocking back and forth, grunting approval. I held her hand, and she held mine.

Our parents, Cuban refugees from the 1960s, chose this run-down art deco hotel on Ocean Drive in South Beach because of its nearness to the sea that held everyone captive. Ours was the Hotel Ocean, two shabby buildings of scuffed walls built closely around a moldy courtyard with a chipped fountain in the center. Marusa lived downstairs from the room I shared with my parents. Across from her lived Ileana and Mayito, twins in my grade at Ida M. Fisher Elementary. While the father worked at the port all day, the mother sat in the living room topless, door open, head thrown back, laughing, acting as if she were fully dressed. What could we say?

Ana María, a grade behind, lived in the other building, upstairs. She said her father refused to leave Cuba when Fidel took over because he couldn't bear to part with their oil paintings: a Rembrandt, a Botticelli, and a few by Wilfredo Lam. Her mother, who now cleaned rooms at a fancy hotel, told everyone it was a matter of time for Cuba to be free, convinced she could reclaim her husband and the artwork at the same time.

Next door to Ana María lived Iraidita, sixteen, thin brown hair down to her knees, who didn't go to school and had a mysterious older sister who went out every night dressed in tight, low-cut dresses, with black eyeliner that reached to her temples, and didn't come home until six in the morning. No one knew her name or where she worked. The sisters were Operation Pedro Pan kids, sent to the United States without parents on a church-sponsored airlift. Iraidita owned a collie, Joaquín, long fur in patterns of white, black, and light and dark brown, with whom she raced every evening at Lummus Park across the street.

A rock wall separated the park from the sand and marked the beginning of the beach where the relentlessly shining sea churned up a neighborhood malaise I couldn't understand. The collie stood without a leash, jumping the wall and coming back, waiting for commands, ears up, until Iraidita threw a stick for him to retrieve. My dog in Cuba never behaved this way, instead running away if not tied up. Marusa III laughed for five minutes when I told her that, clapping her hands at Joaquín from the veranda.

In late afternoon the doctor—everyone called him El Médico, as if he needed no name—spent hours sitting out on the veranda along with his wife and daughter. He read medical books when he wasn't working at Mount Sinai Hospital, sitting by himself in a corner, sometimes glancing up to look at Marusa. He often engaged in conversation with the hotel owners, nicknamed Mudder and Fudder, Yiddish-speaking Holocaust survivors who had bought the hotel after World War II. The old couple nodded at his words, following his gaze to the sea.

The doctor's wife, dressed in flowing flowered dresses, sat nearby, the ocean in her eyes. She took their daughter to school every morning and, after picking her up in the afternoon, walked with her up and down Ocean Drive, the mother pointing out the Tides Hotel, whispering, "See, Margarita? That's where your father and I honeymooned in 1944." When the daughter said she wanted to get home, the mother, face in hands, mumbled she wanted to go home, too.

None of the residents held my attention like Marusa III did. She radiated urgency, inner joy, an indomitable spirit. One day, out on the veranda, when her grandmother wasn't looking, she flung herself out of the chair, hobbled across the street and through the park, climbed over the wall, and made her way on the sand toward the ocean, calling out, "OOO cess." She ran by bracing herself on the left leg, then swinging her right over in an arc to get a foothold while her left propelled her rapidly forward.

"OOO cess," she shouted again. It sounded like the word "lights"—*luces* in Spanish. I gave chase, fear stopping my breath, but Marusa II flew out of the building, leaving me behind in the sand. Fatigue etched her face from a long day working at the school cafeteria. She caught Marusa III at the edge of the sea and dragged her all the way back to the wheelchair, cursing in Spanish while Marusa III tried to explain the unexplainable. Marusa I limped up and down the veranda, hands clasped, calling out to God. Reunited, all three went inside, crying and shouting.

Toward the end of summer, a hurricane thrashed the coastline. Mudder and Fudder called a carpenter to board up the windows facing the sea and nail a plank across the door. We Cubans were unconcerned—hurricanes were commonplace back home—but this one dumped a lot of water overnight, and the sea slapped up over the veranda wall and flooded the lobby.

In the morning everyone ran out to the beach, surveying palm trees bent to the ground like licorice sticks and inspecting piles of sand that had swallowed the stone wall. Parents, worried about losing pay if they couldn't go to work, strolled back to their rooms, hoping the power was on to watch the news.

We children, running over grass and sand, chattered about no school for another week. I raced Iraidita's collie in the park, losing myself in the pleasures of the wind whipping my hair and licking my skin, wishing Marusa III could run with me, the saltwater droplets from the ocean flying into my hair, my mouth, my neck until night fell, a weak moon lighting up a dancing sea. Back at the hotel, I saw the two oldest Marusas standing in a puddle on the flooded veranda, like statues, deaf and dumb, watching the lights of the few ships that made their way up the coast to their northern destinations. The wheelchair stood empty.

"Where's Marusa?" asked Marusa II.

"Maru! Marusita!" The grandmother screamed, awakened from her private daydream.

"She was right here. In this chair!" shouted Marusa II.

Iraidita looked up from the ball she was about to fling across the sand now covering the wall. Her eyes met with a wobbly figure way out in the ocean, lighted by the moon. I followed her gaze. Marusa III's arms flailed once, twice, three times above a wave, and then her head disappeared. Iraidita dropped the ball and sprinted toward the water, Joaquín bounding behind. I ran to the corner of the veranda to get El Médico, sitting in a dry spot, usual chair, reading by flashlight.

"Marusa is drowning," I yelled, tugging at his arm. "Please, please, hurry!" The doctor threw the book down and dashed across the street. I ran close at his heels in the darkness, over the grass of Lummus Park and the sand covering the rock wall all the way to the water. The sand, packed wet from the downpour, made it easier for us to run without it sucking our feet down.

Joaquín stood barking on the shore as Iraidita, out in the water already, struggled to drag in Marusa III, limp in the churning sea. The doctor plunged in and, just in time, snatched the girl from the crest of a wave threatening to sweep her back out. He and Iraidita held tightly to Marusa III as they fought their way back to shore. The doctor swung her up in his arms and laid her on the sand.

"Call an ambulance," the doctor shouted. "Maybe the phones are working."

Iraidita, still trying to catch her breath, ran off with Joaquín at her side.

The doctor straddled Marusa III and forcefully pumped her chest. He grabbed her mouth and placed his over it, blowing as hard as he could. By this time, Marusa I and II reached us, both pulling at their hair. Marusa II sank to her knees and spread out face down on the wet sand, seeming to lose consciousness. Marusa I folded her hands and held them up to the sky, crying: "She wanted to go back to La Habana! God, take me, too!"

The doctor shot her a contemptuous look but kept pumping the girl's chest. A strand of hair hung in his face, another clung to his forehead. Marusa III lay sprawled on her back, right hand curled into her arm, right leg bent at a weird angle, mouth open, eyes open.

I heard the pounding of many feet, everyone in the hotel running to the shore, whispering, moaning, cursing. The doctor looked up. Seawater or tears dripped out of his eyes. He shook his head just slightly. I flung my arms around his shoulders and buried my face in his neck, wailing like Marusa III had on the threshold of that cursed sea, surrendering to my first heartbreak.

To this day I have never quite forgiven my father for not saving my beloved friend.

Mad Magi

On the evening before the early morning fire, Máximo looked up at the black Florida sky littered with diamonds and shivered in the January cold. The wind hurtled off the churning waves in Miami's Biscayne Bay and ripped through his corduroy coat. The links of his 18-carat gold chain felt icy against the coarse hair on his chest. He remembered the winters back home on the island; they were never quite as cold as this one in exile. Not so cold that he had to turn on the electric blanket and plug in the space heater before diving into the sleep that left him feeling more dead than alive.

He reached inside his shirt and touched the carved gold medallion of San Lázaro, patron saint of the sick, the lost, the woebegone, and offered a quick prayer. Standing in the evening wind, he wrestled with the details of a plan growing like a reckless monster in his head. Each time he thought about it, he felt more certain he would go through with it: call Ana from a phone booth, tell her he was ready to leave the family, pick her up at her apartment, and begin the drive north to a new life. There had to be something beyond selling toys seven days a week. He needed lightness of being, and he had to take the first step to find out where it was.

Máximo shivered again and continued his walk toward the Dinner Key Auditorium, where he had set up a kiosk for his Little Havana toy store in an exposition of small businesses. The auditorium, nestled by the water's edge, made a pretty picture against a backdrop of slightly swaying sailboats and yachts moored to the marina. He squared his shoulders as he walked, a muscled man with a light step, hair once thick and black now thinning and graying. Did he have the courage to leave his life behind?

Consider this: When he looked beyond the stars, past the darkness of the marina spilling at the feet of the city's historic Coconut Grove, he did not see the blood of the Cuban Revolution. What appeared before him was his toy store, shoehorned between a greasy cafeteria and a rotting vegetable stand in a row of moldy buildings lining Calle Ocho, Southwest Eighth Street, a dozen or so blocks west of downtown. When he listened for sounds in the stillness, he didn't hear his old neighbors' screams as they slid to the ground before a firing squad. Rather, he heard the sobbing of his wife Marta, five months pregnant, cowering in a corner where he had shoved her. He heard the daybreak arguments of his two older sons, Ignacio and Rolando, who at sixteen and fifteen looked almost like twins, and the arrested laughter of his younger son, Vicente, the happy-go-lucky ten-year-old with stubborn dreams in his eyes and the prison-cell suicide in his future.

He didn't smell the acrid sweat of political prisoners on hunger strikes or those in solitary confinement resisting Fidel Castro by making Christmas cards out of matches in damp, cramped cells. Instead he smelled the pungent aroma of the cafecito hot on the stove, gurgling up like a fountain spray from the lower compartment to spill into the upper. Nor did he taste the blood of a tongue bitten into silence before the deadly harassment of the CDR, the Committee for the Defense of the Revolution. He tasted the sweet guava of the pastelito he dipped into his café con leche. How then, ask yourself, could he support the Cuban counterrevolution from this God-forsaken exile if he was constantly reminded of the material requirements of survival? And, really, how could he think of, no, how could he want anything else except the taste and smell of Ana to help ease the burden?

This very night, from his side of the Florida Straits, he planned to take a bundle of bills from the safe in the store and stash it in his suitcase before he headed out on his journey. His family would not miss the money. For the last few months, after he added up the columns of figures, he saw that his store, Los Reyes Magos, named after the magi who had brought gifts to the baby Jesus in Bethlehem, was making a small profit. At last.

In Cuba, his store had been filled with handmade toys from all over the world. Sales soared right after the Christmas holidays because many children received a second set of gifts on January 6, the Feast of the Epiphany. That tradition was intact among Cubans in Miami, generating brisk sales during the first week of the year just like back home.

Already, eight years after the revolution spurred a mass exodus from the island, Cuban businesses like his were flourishing. Máximo saw the Dinner Key exposition as a collective cry of triumph amid the struggles that characterized life in the 1960s for Cuban exiles. It was a celebration of hard work and another chance at getting back the old, comfortable life. During his early years in exile toiling as a busboy, dishwasher, and gas station attendant, Máximo had saved every penny he could to open his store while making sure his wife and sons ate three meals a day.

Back on the island, he wasn't a millionaire. He was a member of a thriving group of business owners with membership in El Club Nautico, a new Chrysler imported from Detroit, and an apartment in a building called Lago-Mar that overlooked the ocean. Truth be told, he still missed those luxuries. They were closer to becoming reality with last year's booming sales. But somehow, now, they weren't enough.

Months ago, his creative spirit had led him to try his hand at romance novelas that a friend of his published out of a warehouse. He loved the feel of a fountain pen flowing across a crisp white sheet as he composed his stories. Two of them had already hit the newsstands, and, surprisingly, people were scooping them up as fast as the publisher could stock the shelves. Clearly, New York was the place to go with Ana. She said it was the publishing capital of the world! It might be the place for the new start he craved.

Máximo picked up his pace and filled his lungs with the cool, crisp air. He thought of his libido, his main mode of transportation. Without it, he went nowhere. Hadn't he walked away from Ana's bed, still filled with energy, after three rounds of lovemaking? And hadn't he just heard his son whisper to his girlfriend on the phone that his father was un mujeriego, a womanizer? Never satisfied. So? What if he needed the flesh to force the pain from his heart?

What he was planning to do tonight after the bazaar could be the answer to the ever-present malaise. He rehearsed the steps in his mind: drop off any unsold toys at the warehouse, pick up the money at the store, and call Ana. They'd drive to New York in his Corsica. He'd leave the truck for Ignacio and Rolando, who were old enough now—he reasoned—as old as he was when he first went to work on the streets of La Vieja Habana shining shoes. The boys could manage the store and take care of their mother and Vicente. And the new baby? Well, he would send extra money to Marta.

Máximo walked into the brightness of the auditorium and looked around. Businesses of all kinds lined the walls and formed long rows from one end to the other of the building: Islas Canarias restaurant, Suave Shoes, La Epoca women's wear, Librería La Moderna Poesía, Matanzas Hardware and Lumber, García's Jewelry, *El Diario* newspaper. Almost all were transplanted from La Habana.

His eyes rested briefly on the smiling proprietors talking to customers in their kiosks. But the scene dissolved, and in its place he saw a wailing Marta, accusing him of infidelity. He squeezed his eyes shut against the images. He wanted to feel good about his decision. Why couldn't Marta appreciate the discovery of self, the examination of life and culture through conversations? He had had enough of her rejection of his dreams. He often spoke to her in a stream of consciousness, an offering she could not see was the deepest part of him. And when he complained about her lack of attention, why did she always say his concerns didn't have anything to do with her but with his bad feelings about something else? Would it be different with Ana? It was worth a try. Ana understood him.

As Máximo strode up the aisle to his kiosk, his sons ran to greet him. "Papi, estamos vendiendo mucho. ¿Puedes traernos comida al quiosco?" They were selling quite a bit but were hungry and wanted dinner. Marta frowned at him over the shoulders of a couple who had stopped to admire the merchandise. The daughter of Chinese contract laborers brought to the island to work the cane fields, Marta radiated an exotic beauty that had once made him tremble with passion. Once, her slanting eyes and waist-length hair never left his thoughts.

"Está bien," he said, glancing at his wife and noticing the weight gain of pregnancy.

The boys rushed off, and Máximo strolled on through the long aisles to the side of the auditorium where food vendors couldn't keep pace with the demand. He stood in one line and thought about his latest novela waiting for the proofreader at the publisher's office. He had outlined several to be sold in serialized form over a span of a year. Each novela centered on the pain of love, the cruelties of rejection, the desperation of tortured egos scrambling to fill the loneliness.

He pulled a manuscript from his back pocket:

"The union of Ondina and Omar arrived without the

use of words to retract the hurt. Their wordless exchange was reminiscent of the days of pre-language, when primitive ancestors expressed desire in simple ways. And now all the anger, reproach, isolation, and fear of loss rolled up into a cloud of cotton, leaving them sprawled and spent on the floor. The nightmare that had intruded on their lives slipped to the floor like a gown of black velvet."

He put the manuscript away, dissatisfied. He needed to revise. His thoughts of sexual passion, toys, Marta, Ana, and Cuba twisted together in his mind as he ordered arroz con pollo and walked back with the food to his waiting family at the Los Reyes Magos kiosk.

Marta pursed her lips when she saw him but took the bag of food and moved her swollen body over to a table behind the kiosk to serve the hungry boys. Máximo felt her resentment, but what could he do about it? Stop living? It was midnight, the hour when Little Havana residents were most alive. Three more hours to go. His eldest son, Ignacio, bragged about the sales he had closed that evening. Ignacio's girlfriend, Margarita, leaned in a little closer and whispered in his ear. A classmate of theirs, Gerardo, walked over and eyed her up and down. Rolando, Máximo's second son, whistled at a strutting teenaged girl. Vicente, the youngest son, launched into a dance to the beat of a band that had just started up.

"Vamos a dar una vuelta," Ignacio told his father, and Rolando, Vicente, Margarita, and Gerardo followed him, walking over to the band pavilion. Máximo, left alone with Marta, stood up to throw the remains of his dinner in a nearby garbage can. She reached out, a hand on his arm.

"Why?"

"I want everything to be different, everything," he answered, and went after the retreating teenagers.

Suddenly, he saw Ignacio tackle Gerardo to the ground. A flash storm earlier that evening had dumped buckets of water into the auditorium. The boys' heads and legs thrashed around the wet floor, dangerously close to electrical wires submerged in puddles. Ignacio screamed obscenities as he pounded Gerardo. His son's rage sparked memories in Máximo. How many times had he fought for a woman? He wanted to feel the old passion he now saw mirrored in his son's assault.

"Paren ya," he ordered the boys. The two continued to curse, accusing each other of betrayal. Margarita pulled Ignacio away. Gerardo moved in the opposite direction, spitting blood, with Vicente and Rolando chanting, "You lost, you lost."

Máximo stood with the crowd that had gathered at the battle scene, lost in a memory of young love. He remembered that love at first sight had propelled him to a relentless pursuit of a bright-eyed thirteen-year-old he had met at a dance. The day after the party, they sped on bicycles through the twilight to catch the last rays of the sun in a deserted neighborhood park. There, behind the wrought iron fence and under the trees where a carpet of dried leaves felt as soft as down, there, just on the edge of night, they embraced until the moon came up. The next day she told him not to call anymore, that she had a boyfriend.

He squeezed his eyes shut and shook his head to clear the old recurring vision. The crowd was gone. He reached back into his pocket and read the crumpled manuscript aloud: "The roller coaster of love dared Omar to climb aboard. It was the uncertainty of the cars careening on the rails that kept him going back for more. He knew that the death wish was tied closely to his exalted celebration of life." Máximo felt his words ramble without meaning. He knew that tomorrow the proofreader would smirk at his copy as she had done so many times before. He didn't care. He had to keep writing even if he hated what he wrote. Why was he never satisfied with anything?

Each morning in his store, as he stocked the shelves with new toys, he listened to Radio Reloj broadcasting news about the island. Yet another group of exiles was planning an invasion of Cuba. But how could he be in the prime of life and risk death battling Fidel? He couldn't. He wanted to be happy. He had a right. Could he just walk away from the business he had worked so hard to build up, now that it was making a profit? Did he have the courage to escape with Ana to another unknown future? Could he leave Marta and the unborn child?

Why didn't he stay in Miami and work for one of the anti-Castro groups writing press releases to the American media? Why didn't he write novels about Cuba for the readers who so craved his love stories? The island was a shifting memory, fading at times and overpowering at others, but his sad life with Marta was a constant. And now an opportunity for happiness beckoned.

Máximo walked back to the kiosk and spent the next hours ringing up sales while Marta sat heavily in a chair, legs like tree trunks raised on a packing crate. At three a.m. he and his sons packed up the unsold merchandise. He brought his truck to the front and helped Marta climb onto the seat while the boys loaded the crates in the back.

"Are you coming home tonight?" Marta whispered.

He nodded. What else could he do?

Máximo drove to their apartment. He left Marta and the boys on the doorstep and then made his way to the warehouse a mile north and dropped off the toys. Back at the apartment building, he sat in the truck in the parking lot. The bedroom windows were dark. He dismissed regret at not packing a suitcase. He had made a lot of money tonight and could buy a new wardrobe. It was more than enough to leave half for Marta and take the rest for the journey. Ana had a bit of money, too. They would both get writing jobs in New York before it all ran out.

Máximo felt a twinge of anticipation. Maybe hope, happiness? Like him, Ana valued words and the life of the imagination. She was an editor at the novela publishing house. In just a few minutes, he would be speaking to her on the phone.

He got out of the truck and noticed a small open box on the back seat. He had forgotten these ceramic treasures from Spain, delicately painted figurines from a Nativity set. He reached into the box and lifted a tiny tree with steel leaves bursting from the top. He touched the faces of the Magi, Balthasar of Arabia, Melchior of Persia, and Gaspar of India. They had traveled for so long to visit the baby Jesus. What was his journey in comparison to theirs? Nothing. Should he reconsider? The figurines glistened in the light from the streetlamp.

His mind raced back to all the chilly mornings in La Habana when he and his brothers had rushed to the living room to see what the Three Kings had left, a baseball mitt, a bat, a box of dominos. The toys were not new; they were from dusty boxes that someone had donated to the church. Each year, next to the presents, his parents set up a tiny Nativity to remind their sons about the meaning of the holiday, the Feast of the Epiphany. Why was it so important? It had to do with a sudden blast of understanding, a realization of something. Of what? Of what? Nothing came to him but pain, anxiety, as if he were jumping outside of self. Regret. So much regret.

The cold wind prodded him back to the present. His gaze fell on the 1962 silver blue Corsica, the one he bid low for at an auction because it had been in an accident. He had long contemplated driving it into a canal, calling the insurance company and claiming it had been stolen so he could get the money for a new one. How wonderful it would feel to have a new car!

He picked up the box of ceramic figurines and moved them to the front seat of the Corsica. He'd take the set to the store before he fled to carry out his plan. He simply had to have a Nativity set for sale in his store, the holiday quickly approaching. He placed the manuscript in the glove compartment. He slid into the driver's seat, swung out of the lot, and sped in the direction of the store. When he reached Southwest Eighth Street and Twelfth Avenue, he slowed down at the corner. He saw a white cloud ascending. It spread upwards like a claw into the sky. He smelled burned coffee and wondered if someone had already started making breakfast. He smelled burned wood. His eyes narrowed. He smelled burned plastic. He drove closer and stopped. A yellow light moved erratically in the front window of Los Reyes Magos.

He stumbled out of the car and struggled with the keys on his chain. Finally finding the right one, he shoved it into the keyhole and kicked open the door. The flames stretched toward him, licking his skin. He hesitated on the doorstep, mesmerized by the sight of the neatly stocked shelves of toys engulfed by fire. Choking, tears streaming into his mouth, Máximo walked into the heat of the billowing clouds and screamed in anguish. Yes. He had to rebuild. Again. It would be easier this time. And Ana? Couldn't think about her now. This was it. The epiphany.

He made his way to the safe in a corner. This time, his fingers slid without stumbling to open the lock. He scooped up several stacks of bills, held together with rubber bands, and stuffed them into his pockets. Deep under a pile of clean-up rags, he felt for the hidden box. Coughing wildly, he grabbed the rags and held them to his nose and mouth to block the insistent smoke. The flames reached him, elbow and ankle on fire now, ignored. His fingers flicked the top off. The string of pearls winked in a spear of light from a fire column over his head, a Christmas gift for Marta he had not, in his anger, given her. He would take them to her now. Right now. He turned and leaped over a fallen shelf to the front door, his other ankle bright with fire.

The Last Girl

I

The first sunrays crept in like thieves through the iron bars guarding window slits. Sylvia slipped her hand under the pillow, the knife sharp against her forefinger. Down the hall, she heard water from showers and toilets leaking on the floor. Would she make it to the bathroom and back before anyone woke up? Knowing she wouldn't, she shifted on the lumpy mattress and slipped back under the blanket, rough as a Brillo pad against her skin, and waited for the Saturday breakfast bell.

In the three years that she lived at the Florida City Home for Girls, Sylvia had survived cigarette burns, switch-blade slashes, punches and slaps and, one time, a near rape before she managed to run to safety. The bunk beds lined up against the walls held her attackers, the ones to whom she intended to teach a lesson this morning. Leaning on one elbow, brow furrowed, she looked around the stuffy, dank dormitory decorated with rusty hooks sagging under the weight of wrinkled blouses, torn skirts, and patched pants. She had yet to miss the stealthy approach of dawn.

A cool December breeze pushed itself in between the iron bars and stroked her face. Sylvia could stay in bed reading all day if she chose to, as she often did on the weekends, an escape from the weekday classes in the big auditorium, students hurling spitballs, laughing and screaming while a tired teacher ineffectually followed her lesson plan.

At her desk in a corner, Sylvia would shut her mind to the chaos, scribbling scrambled feelings into a notebook. Writing helped her place the pain outside of herself, delaying emotions until she was in bed, memories battling inside her head. She heard her mother shout from the airport runway, "You'll be safe from the communists," and she saw her grandmother, standing next to her mother, slip to the tarmac in a faint, her father struggling to lift her. She saw, too, beaches stretching for miles, a playroom filled with books, arroz con pollo on outdoor tables, her brother playing with Negrito, her parents smiling, herself sitting on her grandmother's lap. The longing never left her. It merged into one big, heavy black void that clung to her lungs, her stomach.

A plume of smoke rising above a top bunk on the other side of the room reminded her of the morning's mission. Fewer attendants were on duty, and the girls often sneaked in cigarettes, pilfered from the cleaning staff.

"Sylvia," whispered Lorisha from the bed below. "Are you awake?"

Sylvia didn't move, but her hand slipped like a snake back under the pillow and gripped the steak knife she had spirited out of the dining room the night before.

"I know you're awake. Let's smoke."

It was the same command every day. When Sylvia said no, Lorisha snapped open her switchblade and brought it close to her neck. Sometimes Lorisha managed to elicit a thin line of blood. "What's wrong wid you, white girl? You think you better 'n us?" She then brought the cigarette close to Sylvia's flesh and pressed down hard. Sylvia had no alternative but to puff weakly from the offered cigarette, her mind shutting off the pain.

Across the room Vanetta jumped out of her bunk and came up to Lorisha with a book of matches in hand. She lit Lorisha's cigarette while holding her own in a corner of her mouth. Lorisha scrambled up next to Sylvia, folded her nightgown around her legs, and leaned back against the wall with the cigarette between her fingers. She inhaled deeply and let the smoke ooze out of her nostrils and mouth into Sylvia's face. Vanetta climbed up beside her. Both girls stared at Sylvia, who stared back.

Lorisha turned to Laverne, who had just walked up, and pressed the tip of the cigarette to hers to light it. Vanetta, Lorisha, and Laverne inhaled and puffed out the smoke, eyes on Sylvia. Around them, the rest of the girls struggled into wakefulness, groaning, throwing sheets and blankets onto the floor, a few running for the showers. Lorisha took her cigarette out of her mouth, leaned over, and brought it close to Sylvia's forearm.

Before she could press it into the skin next to a row of round, almost healed burns, Sylvia threw off Lorisha's hand, whipped the knife out from under the pillow, and jumped to her knees. She held the tip of the knife under

Lorisha's chin and, with the other hand, clutched the girl's hair, pulling back her head. Simultaneously, with a swift leg movement, she kicked Vanetta off the bed.

"Leave me alone, or I'll kill you," Sylvia whispered in Lorisha's ear. Her words were now devoid of the accent she had struggled with that first year, her pronunciation provoking sneers and a string of curse words each time she spoke. "I'm not afraid of you anymore." Sylvia curled her lip to show the tips of her teeth. "Get off of here and never bother me again."

Around the room, the sound of steel switchblades snapping open pierced the low buzz of the morning rush. A door scraped the floor, the knob hitting the wall, and a sleepy attendant appeared in the doorway. Switchblades disappeared under mattresses; Lorisha slid down from Sylvia's bed and, along with Laverne and Vanetta, now off the floor but flinging Sylvia a curse, rushed to gather towels and head for the showers, grinding out their cigarettes on the pocked walls. The attendant, in a light blue uniform and a towel wrapped around her head, ignored the three girls rushing by and walked over to Sylvia, who, body trembling, shoved the knife under the pillow, slumped back, and stared at the ceiling.

"Here," the attendant said. "This came for you."

In crooked cursive, her mother had written out Sylvia's name and the address of the girls' home on the envelope. The letter, dated October 21, 1965—two months ago—from Havana, read:

Querida hijita,

Don't despair. Your father is doing all he can to speed up the exit visas. The Freedom Flights have just started and we're at the top of the list. Your uncle flew your brother from Ohio to live with him now in Miami, gracias a Dios. He could not adjust to the weather, and he was always sick. He even got pneumonia. Your father and grandmother send their love. It won't be long now.

Tu mamá

Sylvia harbored little hope of seeing her parents or beloved grandmother again, or, for that matter, her brother. Immediately after the brother and sister arrived in Miami in the middle of the Cuban Missile Crisis—their flight carried the last of the fourteen thousand Cuban children brought to the city in a covert Washington-backed airlift organized by the Catholic Church and dubbed Operation Peter Pan—harried US officials told fifteen-year-old Renecito that a childless Catholic couple in Toledo had agreed to be his foster parents.

Clasping hands and dazed by the news of another separation, the siblings waited with dozens of children jostling for space in the hall of the Greater Miami Archdiocese's makeshift processing center. Sylvia noticed she was the last girl to be processed. "Girls are a lot more trouble than boys," the eleven-year-old heard a church worker say from behind a desk. "They drop out of school, get pregnant, you know." Maybe watching all the American movies back in Cuba had helped her absorb the meaning of the foreign sounds of English, but in that moment had come other knowledge. She was a girl, alone, unwanted, far from home, a refugee. Longing for her parents burst like a bomb in her heart. She leaned over and threw up the crackers and cheese she had gobbled on the plane.

"Oh my," the church worker exclaimed, and rushed to clean up the mess.

In just forty-five minutes Renecito, trying to look grown up, waved goodbye and walked off to another hall to be processed for his new home in Ohio. Sylvia, along with three other girls, boarded a minibus bound for area orphanages. Her destination: Florida City, forty miles south of Miami. A gray fortlike building entrenched in a forest clearing like a wart in the palm of a hand waited for her. The wooden double doors with medieval steel straps joined ranks with the walls, offering an impenetrable entry and an almost impossible exit. The Home for Girls once served as a World War II army barracks, housing troops in support of the Homestead Air Force Base fifteen miles away. Now the dismal edifice, twenty years after the war, incongruously overflowed with adolescent girls enjoying strenuous play. They waited for adoption, or the legal age of adulthood so they could move out on their own, or, as in Sylvia's case, for a parent who had promised—long ago—to pick them up.

Sylvia folded the letter and pressed it to her heart. *Why couldn't Uncle come to get me to live with him? Why did it have to be Renecito? My parents will never come. I will never leave this place.* She took out a pen and pad from a small box at the foot of the bed. On a clean sheet, she wrote: "My mother doesn't love me." She wrote it nine more times before she placed the pad and letter in the box and covered it with the blanket. She pulled out an old, ragged copy of *Arabian Nights* and stretched out her legs, propping up the book on a pillow.

II

The afternoon that her uncle drove her parents to pick her up at the Home, Sylvia was in bed reading *Hans Christian Andersen's Fairy Tales.* The book was so battered that the pages had come loose from their binding. Volunteer workers from the archdiocese had brought in boxes of old books, and when she picked this one, one of them snapped: "Aren't you too old for fairy tales?" Sylvia had shrugged.

She loved the story "The Wild Swans." A princess delivers her eleven brothers from an evil fate. *I'm as brave and good as she is. If only my mother knew, she wouldn't favor Renecito.* She imagined herself leaving the Home dressed in a beautiful white gown, like the princess, loved at last, flanked by her parents.

Since her act of bravery with Lorisha six months before, she had gained the respect of all the girls. It helped that Lorisha and Vanetta were gone. One had turned eighteen and moved in with an older sister. The other left with her father, who claimed her after a stint in a drug rehab program. Sylvia kept the knife under her pillow. When she went outside, she slipped it inside her knee-highs under her trousers. New girls came in every day, girls with wild expressions, or blank faces. It was hard to tell who were the troublemakers.

This hot, humid summer afternoon, the loudspeaker in the dorm emitted a crackling sound before blasting: "Sylvia, come to the office. Sylvia, come to the office." The words slurred together as if they were all one. Sylvia flung her legs over the edge of the bed and slipped to the floor. As she dressed, the rain outside began again, and the girls playing basketball ran into the building, leaning against the window slits smoking and laughing. Sylvia walked past the bunks and a sagging Ping-Pong table, down a hall, and into the office.

A different Sylvia from the one four years ago paused just inside the door. Slender, dressed in a black skirt and white blouse, she awkwardly pushed back her wavy shoulder-length brown hair. Her gray eyes, the color of wet sand, and her lips, full and red tinged, could have made her face beautiful, but a hard stare and set mouth repudiated beauty. She frowned.

"Sylvia, your parents are here," the director said. "They have come to take you home."

Sylvia didn't immediately see them. From one corner of the room, the church worker who had processed her at the archdiocese locked eyes with her. Sylvia shifted her gaze to the scared-looking couple standing, wide-eyed, to one side. Her uncle sat in a chair, nonchalantly smoking a cigar. Her mother stretched out her arms. Sylvia didn't move. "Sylvita." Her father, his voice ripping like paper, stepped forward. The church worker put up her hand in warning. "It's not unusual for the children to show no emotion," she said. "Everything has changed for them."

"Are you ready to go home?" the director asked.

Sylvia shrugged, her eyes going from her mother to her father and back. *Do they really want me? Why did it take them so long? Where is my grandmother?*

"Go on and pack your suitcase," the director said cheerfully, as if arranging a bowling outing. "Your parents have found a wonderful apartment, and you are going to have your own room."

Sylvia turned and walked back to the dorm. She leaned her head against the mattress, wishing she could climb back up into her bunk and read. *I'm finally leaving. Why don't I feel happy?* She took out the old plastic suitcase from underneath the bunk bed, walked to a chest of drawers, grabbed a handful of clothes donated by the church, and threw them inside. She picked up the books she had brought from La Habana, *El León Famélico*, *El Nuevo Bebé*, *Señor Perro*, and packed them away, along with the English books and the box containing her notebook. She took up a green plastic rosary that glowed at night and a small catechism book and left them on her pillow. She walked back up the hall, balancing the suitcase, and paused at a window. One of the new girls threw a faded basketball at a rusted, crooked hoop tied to a lamp post. The ball bounced off and landed in a rain puddle, splashing the screeching girls with cold sprays of water.

On the way to their new home Sylvia's parents kept up a steady chatter with her uncle.

"There's no food in Cuba," Elena said. "We stand in line for hours for a cup of rice."

"We did the right thing getting the kids out when we did," Rene said. "All the children now belong to the state. They're forced to study what the government chooses."

"Thank God for the Freedom Flights," Elena added, "or we would still be back in Havana."

"You're going to miss Cuba after a while," Ambrosio said. "You'll see. But now you have to focus on working."

Sylvia remembered Ambrosio from family dinners, remembered him chewing on a thick cigar, eating greasy pork rinds and gulping down beer. He wore freshly starched white guayaberas—linen shirts elaborately pleated in the front—and drove a brand-new Chevrolet. He was her mother's rich brother, who left Cuba at the start of the revolution, taking with him bundles of cash before the new "caudillo," Fidel Castro, froze bank accounts on the island.

"We've never worked in a factory," Elena said. "We're office administrators!"

"Here you have to start at the bottom unless you come with money," Ambrosio said. "It's not hard stitching soles on shoes with the machines they have. It's temporary until you get on your feet."

"I can probably be a manager there in no time," Rene said.

Ambrosio turned into the driveway of a small building in a neighborhood that would soon be called Little Havana and shut the motor. He ran up a steep flight of exterior stairs to the second floor. Rene took Sylvia's suitcase and started the ascent. His once black hair, still thick, gleamed in the sun. His light blue eyes, framed in horn-rimmed glasses, turned to smile at her. She averted her gaze. On the sidewalk, her mother, who Sylvia remembered as tall and beautiful, now heavyset with hair that looked as if she had cut it herself, held out her hand to her daughter, but Sylvia pretended not to notice. At the top of the stairs, just outside the apartment door, she saw her grandmother leaning on a cane, hand shaking on the handle, almost unrecognizable. Gone were the sparks from her blue eyes, much darker and more alive than Sylvia's father's, her once flowing white hair now unevenly cropped close to the head.

"Mi nietecita," Elvira said in a sobbed whisper when Sylvia stood before her. She grasped Sylvia around the neck with one arm. The smell of Violetas Rusas, a popular Cuban cologne mainly used on babies, filled Sylvia's nostrils, and she stepped back, disgusted, almost stumbling back down the stairs, love fighting its way back into her heart but blocked.

"Be careful," Elvira gasped.

"Abuela!" Sylvia shouted, and, exasperated, gained her footing and disengaged herself from the embrace. The word lingered in the air as her father shuttled off to a side room to deposit the suitcase and her mother went into the kitchen to prepare a cafecito, sugared espresso.

"She's tired," her mother said. "She's gone through a lot."

"Sylvita," Elvira said, but Sylvia turned her back. It had become an involuntary act to move away from people speaking to her.

"I understand you," the old woman said. "Your pain

must melt away, so you can begin to live again. You are a young girl. You will recover."

"¿Y Renecito?" Sylvia asked, looking around the apartment. The small sitting room stretched into an even smaller dining room, with a slip of a kitchen behind a wall. Two bedrooms opened out from the front room.

Elena paused. "He's in Tallahassee working at a college internship," she answered. "He couldn't come to meet you, but he'll be here during the school break in December."

"That's nice. I guess I'm too much trouble to be considered for anything."

"Don't say that. You too can go to college," Elvira exclaimed. "And you have your family now."

"Where's my room?"

"You're sharing with your grandmother," her father said, apologetically. "We couldn't afford anything bigger than this place."

The Home director had lied, or maybe her parents had forced the administrator to lie.

"I won't make any noise in the room," Elvira whispered. A strand of hair fell, defeated, on her forehead. Sylvia remembered how her grandmother bought her books and read to her, leaping to her defense when her parents punished her as a child. But that was another world. Pushing away the memory, Sylvia felt no connection to anyone in the apartment.

"I have to go," Ambrosio announced, stepping toward the door. "The grocery store is two blocks away. The school is five blocks away. Sylvia can walk there. I'm still working on getting a good deal on a used Ford for you, Rene.

You start work on Monday. I'll pick you up early." He moved over to Sylvia and bent down to kiss her. Sylvia dodged him.

"Which room is it?" she asked. "I want to read now."

III

Elvira slipped out the prayer card from the missal she kept by the bed and stood up. It was Sylvia's sixteenth birthday, and she had all the ingredients ready to bake a cake, but the arthritis in her hip shot arrows of pain down her thigh to her knee. She caught her breath and put her hand over her mouth to stop the sharp cry forming in her throat. She didn't want to wake Sylvia. She eased her body back onto the sheets and prayed.

"Jesús, todo poderoso," Elvira began, "help my granddaughter."

Outside, the clatter of breakfast dishes echoed through the apartment. Rene and Elena woke up at dawn to get ready for work. Sylvia, on summer vacation, stayed up all night reading and didn't wake before noon. After a quick lunch, she went back to bed and read some more. Luckily, Elvira thought, school would start next month and end her granddaughter's inactivity and depression.

Elvira moved a pile of books on the night table to clear space for her to lean. *Gone with the Wind. Forever Amber. Rebecca.* She had bought them for Sylvia from the Book of the Month Club with money from her refugee aid check. The pain jabbed her waist, her back, her leg. She took up a brace from the floor, bent down slowly, pushed her toes inside, and pulled up the contraption. She grimaced, lips sealed against her teeth. Last year, a mild stroke had left her right foot limp and unresponsive. The brace kept her foot up and in place but pinched her ankle and bruised her shin. She couldn't bear the disgust on Sylvia's face when she dragged her foot as she walked. Elvira tied the two straps together in front of her leg and leaned back on her hands to rest. After a moment, she took up her cane and pushed herself to her feet.

"I hate you. I hate you," she heard Sylvia scream from the living room.

Startled, Elvira glanced at the bed next to hers. It was empty.

"What's fifty dollars?!" Sylvia yelled. "If I take this writing course, I can get a job at a newspaper and move out. You don't want me here. All you care about is Renecito!"

Elvira limped to the door.

"I don't have time to argue," her mother answered.

Rene came out drying his face with a towel.

"No more arguments," he said. "Your grandmother is going to cook a special dinner for your birthday, and then we're going to the drive-in tonight."

"I don't want to eat dinner with you, and I don't want to go to the drive-in in that old car. I'm tired of being in the same room with Abuela. She stinks. She pees in her pants."

Her mother took up her purse, and her father grabbed his keys.

"It's a year already that you've been out of that Home, and you haven't changed one bit," Rene said, his face lined with fatigue. Without eating breakfast, her parents descended the stairs.

"You don't care about me," Sylvia yelled.

"You are impossible," Elena hurled back.

Elvira glanced at the Sacred Heart of Jesus on the prayer card, steadying herself with the wall. *They don't give her enough love. Not enough attention. Today, I'm going to give her my pearl earrings, the ones I got when I was fifteen. I don't blame her. If only she could remember me as I used to be.* Elvira slowly made her way out of the bedroom and into the kitchen.

"Buenos días," she said.

Sylvia didn't answer, adding and subtracting busily in a notebook, her head bent low over the figures.

Elvira filled the coffee pot with water, placed it on the stove, sliced a loaf of Cuban bread, and positioned two thick chunks in the oven. She turned and took down the flour and sugar from the cupboard.

"I don't want breakfast, and I don't want a cake, Abuela."

Outside, thunder growled in the morning sky. From the window, Sylvia watched the sun stab weakly through the narrow spaces between gray clouds. The news said a hurricane was treading water off the coast of Cuba, meandering its way toward the Florida Keys. Sylvia closed her notebook, donned a bathing suit, and ran down the stairs. In the back of the building, next to a small murky pool, Sylvia placed an old towel on a plastic lounge chair. Ignoring the threat of lightning, she applied baby oil on arms, legs, face, and neck. Green muck hugged the edges of the pool. Palm fronds floated in the deep end. Sylvia had not slept all night, but she wasn't tired. The argument with her parents had energized her. She extended her arms above her head and dove deep. She arched her back and paddled to the surface, climbed up, and stretched out on the lounge chair.

My parents will never have any money for me to go to college. Will Uncle help me like he did with Renecito? No, and I don't care. I will do everything for myself. I'll get a job and save. She turned her head and spied the mail truck around the corner. Wrapping the old towel around her waist, she rushed out to meet the mailman. He smiled at Sylvia, but she didn't smile back. As soon as he closed the mailbox door, she opened the broken steel flap and reached inside, drawing out a letter from the Famous Writers School.

Sylvia tore open the envelope and read swiftly:

Dear Miss Lopez,

We are pleased to inform you that your entrance examination demonstrated that you have great talent and a bright future ahead. We particularly liked your use of similes and metaphors.

Enclosed please find a contract specifying the terms of the school. As soon as we receive your check, we will mail you the packet. Welcome to the Famous Writers School, where every writer is a published writer!

Sylvia breathed hard. *I need the money now! There is a box of coins on top of my parents' closet and maybe Abuela can give me some of her government check.* She started up the stairs, now slippery with the first drops of rain.

Elvira limped out of the bedroom with the box of pearl earrings and made it all the way to the landing just as Sylvia reached the top step.

"Abuela, I'm going to be a famous writer."

"You are? How?"

"I have to take lessons. Please, Abuela, I need fifty dollars. Look, the school accepted me." She handed Elvira the letter although her grandmother could not read English.

"My dear, you know the money is needed for food, for rent."

"But, Abuela, these lessons will help me get a writing job. I could pay you back. I could even help out Mami and Papi. Please, please!"

"Maybe Ambrosio can help you get a loan."

"He won't. I hate him."

The stench of urine reached Sylvia as Elvira moved closer, away from the door, one hand shaking on the cane and the other gripping a small jewelry box and the letter. Out on the landing, with the breeze cooling the rain on her face, Sylvia felt lightheaded. A wave of nausea made her stomach contract. She met her grandmother's eyes, filled with love and compassion, and noticed a cloudy film covering the pupils. Elvira's hair was oily and parted in odd places, revealing a pink scalp, like the skin of a white pig Sylvia had seen once on a farm near the Home for Girls. Sylvia hated the animal on the spot, and she climbed back on the bus, refusing to leave her seat during the entire field trip. She hated the pig for being defenseless, weak, and for not knowing it was about to be slaughtered.

Sylvia took a step toward the door, rage rising. Elvira

rotated out of the way and moved closer to the stairs, her back now against the light. She looked suspended in air, with the flight of stairs spilling behind her down to the sidewalk like a braid of long hair. Wobbling on the cane, surprised at the anger pulsating from Sylvia's face, Elvira stepped backward. Her foot slipped on the wet tile.

Sylvia lunged forward and grasped her grandmother's dress, but the old woman's weight ripped the cloth from her hand. Elvira floated out of Sylvia's reach; her eyes locked on her granddaughter's, registering a moment of recognition, as if she remembered something that had eluded her for days. She tumbled down the stairs, step by step, until she reached the bottom.

"Abuela, Abuela!" Sylvia yelled, running down after her.

Kneeling on the grass, she scooped up the old woman's almost weightless, broken body and pressed it close to hers. She shed—in the steady rain now pummeling her face and shoulders—all the tears she had held back since she left the island. A gust of wind blew away the letter. The tiny box of earrings lay abandoned on the sidewalk.

Summer of My Father's Gun

"It's loaded," my father said, shoving his silver-and-black handgun with the gold trigger into its leather pouch and placing it on a left-behind glass-topped dining table he had dragged in from someone's trash. "Saved me from being mugged at a gas station," he said, "and it may save you one day."

He took the handgun, hidden in the pouch, everywhere he went. It rested in the car's glove compartment as he drove and on the night table as he slept. Constant, secure, solid. Everything he was not. Of charm and quick wit, he had plenty, and I, an adolescent girl in the mid-sixties, already knew I had to emulate my father to survive.

That summer day my father stood, self-satisfied, gun pouch on the table, in the new home he thought would solve all our problems; thumbs looped into his belt, he surveyed a dozen cardboard boxes the movers had dumped in the middle of our living room. He had reason to feel proud. Just a few years an immigrant, he had achieved the American dream of home ownership, even if the down payment had come from the settlement of my mother's car accident.

With his olive skin, hooked nose, and bedroom eyes, my father could pass for an Arab. "Somebody stopped me at the airport and asked me if I was a sheikh from Iran," he once joked when he was rich, owned a collection of rifles, and wore a diamond on his pinkie finger. But in 1965 he, the son of an office worker, was only a Cuban refugee, one of thousands fleeing to Miami from a Caribbean communist island, hiding a heart longing for wealth he might never have known in his birth land.

"This neighborhood is a lot like Cuba," my mother said with forced cheerfulness, glancing at the gun, "and not that far from the beach." Fragile, graceful, she had a cloud of dark hair and eyes like open wounds. Her mouth split into a grin that spoke of ancient tragedies. Fair skinned, she was the granddaughter of Spanish immigrants who had set up a sugar plantation in Cuba in the mid-1800s. Unlike my father, she had been sheltered from hard work and the stress of economic survival. Now, cultural displacement sent her into a depression she never could evade. She slit open the top of a box with a knife, pulled a pile of monogrammed towels and embroidered sheets from its depth, and dropped them next to the handgun on the table.

"It's safe from hurricanes," my father added, pointing to yellow-striped window awnings poised to close their lids to keep out wind and flying objects.

"And there's a ballet school on the main road," my mother brightly exclaimed, lifting out a cut-glass decanter from which she had once served her guests fine French liqueurs at dinner parties in La Habana.

"Not for me," I said, flicking my fingers over the gun pouch on the table before digging into a beat-up box that held a big gray radio, cracked in one corner from a fall. I wrestled the heavy plastic oblong onto the ledge above a marble fireplace framing an electric heater resembling wooden logs. I found an outlet and plugged the radio into the wall. Sam the Sham sang "Wooly Bully," and my feet flew into a combination of the Twist and the Mashed Potato.

"Soon this area will be called Little Havana," my father shouted over the music.

And it would, becoming a world-famous ethnic enclave known for its anticommunist Cubans. But not just yet: the sensual South Florida landscape hung like a portrait watching over the area's transformation. Just north of Southwest Eighth Street—the hub of Cuban business and political life—and south of impoverished black communities, my new home belonged to a Miami working-class neighborhood in transition: tired and retired northerners and midwesterners who wished for quiet, trying to make sense of the noisy young Cubans moving in.

The music from the radio drifted into the street. I ran out and zigzagged between the trees in the front yard, the backyard, the wind in my face and raindrops as big as quarters kissing my naked shoulders. Rebellious underground tree roots pushed up sidewalk slabs, tripping kids on bicycles. In the humid heat that made breathing difficult, gardenia bushes and mango trees kept the air sweet.

My father followed me into the flash storm to flag down the furniture truck he had seen through the window. Fresh from his residency at Mount Sinai Hospital, he had used a week's pay as a physician's assistant to buy a green couch, two yellow armchairs, and a master bedroom suite. Nothing was too expensive for this new opportunity to forget the past.

On that first day in our new home, after four long years in the crumbling, termite-infested but once-magnificent art deco apartment building on South Beach, my constantly quarreling parents filled the house with hope. While my father told the movers where to place the furniture, my mother stocked the kitchen shelves with English china. On one counter she lined up fancy highball glasses imprinted with Toulouse-Lautrec posters. On another she set out a sterling silver tray with ornately curved feet she later pawned for painkillers and tranquilizers.

Like many families straining toward breakup, we set aside the pain and clung to the freshly painted two-bedroom bungalow with wall-to-wall carpeting and central air conditioning as our lifeline to happiness. On moving day, how could we imagine that—like many of our neighbors up and down the two blocks of our tight little circle—we were beyond repair? Inside the circle struggled a mixture of old-timers and newcomers trying to make sense of a world shaken by an immigration bombshell.

The Smiths

Handwoven tapestries covered the living room walls in

Mrs. Smith's gabled American colonial across the street. "I did them myself," she said, pointing proudly, when—locked out of my house—I knocked on her door to ask for a glass of water. Tall, white hair collected in a net at the nape of her neck, Mrs. Smith handed me the glass and limped to the window. Outside, neighborhood kids kicked a ball around and chased each other, whooping and hollering.

Mrs. Smith wrenched the window open. "Be quiet," she yelled.

Her yell roused Mr. Smith, wrapped in a light blanket and sitting in a wheelchair, from a morning nap. He stared at me and followed my gaze to an oversized framed photograph on a beat-up piano.

"Those are my kids," he said. "The Lord took them in a car accident."

I drew in a quick, shocked breath.

"You Cuban?" he demanded, pointing at me with his chin.

"No. I mean, yes."

"Why are all you people coming over here for? It's beautiful in Havana. The music! The casinos! The night-clubs! I remember them well."

"This child wouldn't know anything about that, Fred!"

Unable to fathom the political intricacies of our island, the Smiths kept their distance. They were tired of life but afraid of death, and along with the other Anglo neighbors, they formed a framework of stillness around the noise in the Cuban houses. Behind their doors they were watchful, peeking out behind a curtain at the slightest sound in the street. In 1950, some of them had vacationed in Varadero

Beach and even danced at the Tropicana; in 1959, they had watched the black-and-white newsreels of Fidel triumphantly entering La Habana; in 1961, they tuned in to see film of the Bay of Pigs invasion; in 1962, with the nation on the brink of nuclear war, they watched footage of the Missile Crisis. Now, in 1965, the news showed dozens of "Freedom Flights" beginning to bring in tens of thousands of refugees.

"Didn't Fidel Castro liberate Cuba from a dictator?" Mrs. Smith asked when I handed back the empty glass. "Isn't he teaching the poor how to read? Doesn't that improve your country?" I didn't know the answer, so I shrugged and slipped back outside to join the ball players. When I told my father, he advised me to say: "Fidel's a communist."

Under his breath, "Stupid Americans."

Mr. McCoy

The widower lived at the top of the slope in a two-story gray house with a red brick chimney. Nobody knew his name—that is, until I asked him. Gossip had it that he went crazy after his wife died. He boarded up his front windows as if he, too, were waiting to die. Dozens of cats lounged on the sidewalk, lawn, porch, and roof. The Animal Control officers came out once and spoke to him, but nothing changed.

On Halloween, that first year of home ownership, a group of us kids knocked on the man's door. "Trick or treat," we yelled, and waited for him to come out on the porch. On a dare, I summoned up the courage to speak as he emerged from the dark house.

"What's your name?" I asked, holding out my bag.

"Jim McCoy," he said, handing out candy.

We stood motionless, taken aback by the sound. I was surprised at the rich, very-much-alive tone of his voice. I peeked out of the eyeholes on my angel mask and saw a form dressed in black, with a beard covering skin whiter than eggshells, the whites of his eyes streaked with yellow. The old man took a step forward.

"Let's get out of here," mumbled my friend Marilyn, who lived next to the Smiths.

I ran, following the group of trick-or-treaters down the stairs of his porch to the next house. But the widower's mournful expression remained in my mind. It reflected the sadness in my own heart, a nagging hurt over the ever-present tension between my parents, the screaming, the accusations, and the silences all rolled up into that dizzying feeling of grief when my father didn't come home and my mother cried all day. But at the core of my child's suffering a thin thread of steel began to emerge; the strength I saw emanate from my father had captured my imagination, and it meant I, too, could do as I wanted. I, too, could think for myself.

Mrs. Locklear and Mrs. White

Mrs. Locklear lived next door in a house painted pink inside and out, including the awnings. Her wide hips swayed powerfully when she walked. Mrs. White, who lived on our other side—in a pink duplex— sat in Mrs. Locklear's living room drinking hot tea on the day we visited. She smiled at us politely, eyes not focusing. Two Siamese cats jumped up onto the couch and curled themselves around her.

The women had been the first to move into the neighborhood thirty years ago. Their husbands had died, and their children had grown up and left home for jobs up north. Unlike the Smiths across the street, the two tried to befriend my mother, without success.

That day, my mother resolved to make it clear why she rejected their overtures. Standing just inside Mrs. Locklear's door, my mother threw her shoulders back and eyed the widows coldly. "I don't want you to talk to us anymore," she said in a soft, almost imperceptible accent. She was the only Cuban woman on the block who spoke English, because she had gone to school in Canada and Boston before teaching the language back home. Wearing dark glasses that hid eyes swollen from all the crying, she looked glamorous, like Jacqueline Kennedy, in a blue knit Chanel suit and white patent leather pumps with bows on the toes. I had my diary and a book under my arm, ready to escape if things got boring during the visit.

Mrs. Locklear, an imposing figure with a booming voice practiced in the art of protest, walked to the back and slammed shut the inner door, complaining the screen door never shut out the mosquitoes. Heavy curtains hung at the windows. Thick pink area rugs covered the floor. Shelves displaying glass figurines lined the walls from ceiling to floor. In the backyard, fruit trees oozed a sugary steam into the heat of the day, and their pungent odor mixed with the air inside. Each night, before going to sleep, I smelled the sweetness, and when I woke up from burglar nightmares, the odor still filled the room.

"I don't know what I have done to offend you," Mrs. Locklear said to my mother, who did not move from her position by the front door. "All I said yesterday was that you can count on me if you need anything. It's the neighborly thing to do."

"I don't need your help. You are friends with them, the ones who want to make trouble for me. They come to my window at night."

"Who are you talking about?"

"You know who I mean."

The widows said nothing.

"Let's go, Margarita. These two want to poison me."

She pivoted smoothly on her heel, and I followed, frowning, frightened. Being with my mother felt like running after an elusive flicker of light in the dark. When the light sparkled from her eyes, I ran to her with arms open. Most of the time, the light disappeared before I could reach her, and I plunged back into darkness. This was one of those dark times. I strained to make sense of things but couldn't. I wanted my mother to be free of her tormentors. Mrs. Locklear and Mrs. White wiggled their fingers at me in a sign of goodbye as I turned to look at them before closing the door.

The Kellys

If Mrs. Kelly once had been poor, she was no longer. The first Cuban in the neighborhood, she moved in fifteen years ago and straddled the divide between the old Anglos and the young Cubans. Her house looked different from everybody else's—newer, more expensive. Huge square rocks in brown, yellow, and gray decorated the front wall.

The double door, painted dark green, sported a shiny brass knocker. Her garden held a profusion of carefully clipped rosebushes and red and purple bougainvillea. Her last name used to be Gonzalez, but when she married John Kelly she became Mrs. Kelly. She chatted only with the old-timers, ignoring all of us Cubans.

"Hi, I have your order," I said to her, holding out a bag filled with Avon cosmetics. Each month she ordered three or four tubes of lipstick and several bottles of nail polish, perfume, and hand cream from Concha, Marilyn's mother. Concha hired me as a delivery girl. Once Mrs. Kelly tipped me a few dimes, and I gave them to my mother.

"Thank you," Mrs. Kelly said as she handed me a stack of dollar bills, took her packages, and closed the door. Through the window, I watched her go into the kitchen to knead a lump of dough resting on the counter. She carried a glass filled with an amber-colored liquid that she drained in one gulp before beginning her task. From the side-walk, I often watched her clean, cook, and garden. In the late afternoons, with glass in hand, she greeted her hus-band, who wore suit and tie and carried a briefcase, at the door with smiling mouth outlined in lipstick just like June Cleaver in the TV show *Leave It to Beaver*.

"Mrs. Kelly is Americanized," Concha told me.

At home, I asked my mother what that meant.

"La senora Kelly has been in this country a long time. She is from a Cuban migration in the fifties," my mother explained. That morning she vacuumed energetically. A small light flickered in her impenetrable black eyes. "She is an economic immigrant. We are not. We are exiles."

"Why are we different?" I jumped at my mother's rare focus, fighting the urge to run toward the light in her eyes.

"Her family left Cuba because of poverty. They came to America to make money. We left because Fidel—¡ese maldito!—wanted to take our money and our freedom. We didn't come here for money."

The light still shone. I didn't dare move, hoping it wouldn't fade.

In the Kellys' backyard, Danny and Joey—about my age—splashed in a plastic pool five feet deep, the only pool in the neighborhood. They didn't go to the local school, but to one far away. Concha said that Danny was different from us, and that his condition caused Mrs. Kelly to have that glass in her hand. Danny was deaf and mute; he had been born that way.

"Hey, you want to go swimming?" Joey yelled as I walked to the next house on my delivery rounds. Danny made distorted sounds with his throat and waved wildly.

"No, thank you." I was tempted, but Danny's handicap repelled me. Mrs. Kelly frowned from the window. In the driveway, a brand-new automobile gleamed in the sun.

Enrique

Every Cuban in the neighborhood wanted to go back to the island, especially Enrique. He was my best friend Marilyn's father, a short, stocky man with black hair slicked back with grease. He lived with his wife, two daughters, and two nieces in the house next door to the Smiths.

"We're only here for a few more months," he said to

his wife, Concha, who sat in the front room staring at the wall. "Cuba will be liberated soon. Fidel will die!"

On the weekends, men in faded pants and wrinkled shirts with hair uncombed and faces unshaven filled his house. Maps dangled from smudged tape on the walls, and piles of papers covered the couch, tables, and floor.

"¡Eres un bruto!" Enrique shouted into the phone, walking up and down rapidly, the cord keeping him on a short rein. Usually a jolly man with deep laugh lines, Enrique pulled at his hair with his free hand. Concha didn't move. Turquoise eye shadow covered her eyelids, and hot pink lipstick spread unevenly across her mouth.

Marilyn, the oldest daughter, wore a grim expression as we played jacks on the floor. Her sister Maritza and cousin Aurora, both a few years younger, watched silently as we bounced the ball and placed one jack on top of the other before sweeping them into our hands. Eighteen-year-old Felicia, Aurora's sister, polished her nails. In the early evening, blasts of air from gyrating fans cooled us off.

Enrique slammed down the phone and joined Concha on the couch, papers slipping off. Another man, sitting on a stool, began the latest rehash of the Bay of Pigs invasion. The world had largely forgotten that more than four years ago in April of 1961, some fifteen hundred Cuban exiles backed by the United States landed in an inlet called Bahía de Cochinos on the southern coast of Cuba. They confidently intended to overthrow Castro, but President Kennedy's promised air cover didn't materialize. In less than twenty-four hours, the exiles surrendered to Castro's forces. The botched attack never stopped taking center stage in Cuban conversations.

"That hijo de puta Kennedy," exclaimed a man squinting at a map on the wall. "It was all his fault. We would be back in Cuba today had he not chickened out at the last moment!"

"We will never give up our dream," another man shouted.

Enrique jumped up from the couch and ran over to another map. "If we landed on the east coast and surprised them here," he said, tracing a route with his finger, "we could get into the interior undetected." As the strategist of the group, he formulated paramilitary exercises the men carried out deep in the marshland of the Everglades where they trained to invade Cuba.

"Los comunistas are on alert wherever there's a harbor," answered someone. "We wouldn't be able to get away with it."

To my parents, just like Concha and Enrique, the island was a stubborn passion impossible to ignore. To me, it meant speaking Spanish with them and English with my friends and both languages at the same time when I wasn't thinking. It meant writing letters to my grandmother, step-grandmother, and great-uncle back in La Habana. But mainly it meant I had rhythm when I shook my hips and shoulders to a danzón at the Dinner Key Auditorium on New Year's Eve.

Was I Cuban or American? Maybe this move to a new house would help me figure it out. I pondered the question as I watched Enrique stash guns in the rickety storage shed in his backyard, convinced his group would liberate Cuba. Did I want to go back? No. Enrique was certain we would. My father said Enrique wasted his time. "Cubans are here to stay," he said. "We have no choice but to work hard and rebuild our lives."

The year before, I later learned, Castro had signed a sugar trade agreement with the Soviet Union, the island's main military and commercial ally, lassoing Cuba securely to the United States' giant communist enemy, dimming some exiles' hopes for a return. Not Enrique's. "The Cuban embargo will help us win," he said, "but our guns and brave men must be ready."

I didn't care about politics, and the memories of my home in La Habana were quickly fading, supplanted by this to-me-luxurious house where I could dig my toes into the thick carpet. If only my parents would stop fighting, everything would be perfect. All I wanted was to read in the breeze outside under a leafy tree canopy and to write stories in my diary in my pink-curtained room. But by the time I started writing this story, all hope of having a happy family had vanished.

My Father

Nothing could hold him. Not our new house, my beautiful mother, or his growing daughter. Just weeks after the year slipped away—with no celebration of Thanksgiving or Noche Buena, though I did get a record player for Christmas—and I turned twelve, my father announced he had a new job at Edgewater Hospital in Chicago. "It's a good opportunity," he said. "No one is hiring Cuban doctors in Miami, so I have to leave to make a living."

He bought thermal underwear and a long, thick

woolen coat from the Sears catalog. In March he was ready to go. "We'll be together again," he promised. "You can move to Chicago as soon as I'm settled, and your mother rents the house."

One morning before dawn he jumped in his car, waved goodbye, and drove off. I stood at the door watching the lights of his car dissolve into the night, like a lump of white sugar in black coffee. I walked back to my room. The furniture painted in cream and gold leaf in the style of the French king Louis XV looked old in the darkness. A soft pink flowered spread draped the bed. Heavy satin curtains blocked out the light of the streetlamps. I took up my father's picture from the night table and pressed the frame to my heart.

"Querida Margarita," my father wrote in the first letter. "It hasn't stopped snowing since I got here. I have an apartment around the corner from the hospital. It's very small. I'm not sure yet when you'll be able to come. I miss you so much. Lots of kisses. Tu papi."

Margarita

I was afraid to be in the house alone with my mother. Next-door neighbor Mrs. Locklear didn't try to relieve my fears. "A month before you all moved in," she said, with a twist to a mouth centered between two sagging cheeks, "a burglar crept into your kitchen through the back door. But the house had an alarm and the burglar ran away." I knew we had no alarm. If only my father had left his gun behind!

For weeks I stayed awake at night thinking about what

I would do if another burglar sneaked into our house. I made up different escape routes in my mind and went over them again and again. I pictured myself jumping out the back window and running for help or hiding in the closet or crawling underneath the bed. I told my mother my plans and begged her to lock her bedroom door each night before going to sleep, just in case. She laughed the laugh of darkness and shook her head.

But then a miracle happened: I found my father's gun. Had he left it behind on purpose? Did my mother steal it from him and hide it? Whatever the circumstances, I could sleep again.

Concha

Marilyn's mother loved her husband one day and hated him the next. Everybody on the block heard her yell at Enrique late into the night. In the morning, Concha passionately embraced him on the porch before he rushed to work at a body shop on Southwest Eighth Street.

Concha dressed in black every day now. Her uncle in Cuba had died. During the day, she packed Avon cream, perfume, lipstick, eye shadow, and blusher in plastic bags for her customers. After school, girls in the neighborhood helped her check each item off a list. Then we would deliver them to nearby houses, bringing back payments from the customers.

One time, as we sorted through new colors of eye shadow, the whimpers of Marilyn's younger cousin Aurora slipped past the closed door as she cowered in her room. "Mi mamá," I heard her cry softly. "I want my mother!"

Aurora's mother, Concha's sister, waited in Cuba for an exit visa to the United States. Fearful for her daughters' futures, she had sent her girls to Concha in an emergency airlift of fourteen thousand children called Operation Peter Pan.

I stood up from the table and tiptoed to the entrance of Aurora's room, back flat against the wall, and watched Concha walk toward the little girl with belt in hand.

"¡Eres mala!" Concha yelled: Aurora was bad. "I told you to put the dishes in the sink." Concha swung the belt across Aurora's back. The girl started to crawl underneath the bed, but Concha grabbed her legs and pulled her out. I averted my eyes, feeling lightheaded, and thought about the gun at home. Would this be a good time to use it? Maybe just to scare Concha a little?

"I can't stand it anymore!" Concha yelled. "I can't take it alone all day with these four girls." She threw the belt into a corner and crumpled to her knees; her fingers dug into her scalp. "What am I going to do? I'm going crazy. ¡Loca! ¡Loca!"

I tiptoed back to the family room. Marilyn and Maritza, faces closed, packed cosmetics. Aurora's sister, Felicia, wept. If any of the girls spoke at times like this, Concha would slap her across the face.

"Felicia has to get married," Marilyn whispered. "We can't afford to keep her or Aurora anymore, and they don't know if their mother is ever going to come from Cuba."

Rosa

Rosa lived in the shadows, in a tiny 1920s house with dingy coral rock walls in what was called the Spanish style, set far

back from the street, between Mrs. Locklear and the old widower McCoy. Tall trees with thick trunks and branches bent
to the ground formed a curtain of green and brown in the
front yard, providing a delightful hiding place. The coarse
vegetation dripped with water not burned off by the sun.

When I looked at Rosa, she appeared as if through
a soft mist. Red-brown freckles painted a delicate design
over her creamy white face. Her eyes, shaded by stubby
black lashes, reflected the red in her hair and face. She was
eighteen, like Felicia, but while Felicia stayed home cook-
ing and cleaning, Rosa drove every day to a nearby college
in the family's rusty Ford Starliner.

"Do you want to see my books?" I asked her, trying to
get her attention as she backed out of her driveway.

"I can't. I have to go to the library."

"I want to go to the library, too. I love to read and to
write."

"It's very important to study a career. My father says
that if he had a college education we wouldn't be living in
this smelly old house. We have no air conditioning, the
refrigerator leaks on the floor, and the stove doesn't work."

"My air conditioning broke, too," I said, surprised at
her emotion. "It's really hot, but we have fans."

"We don't have money for fans," Rosa answered,
making the motor roar. "I hate it here!" She sped off, car
lurching.

Margarita

The Smith and Wesson rested in an old cardboard box in

the closet, on top of my mother's photo albums, from back in her great-grandparents' time, preserving the monied past in which she had lived. I lifted out the familiar leather pouch and pulled open the zipper, revealing the sleek black-and-silver handgun with the gold trigger. I slipped my fingers around the short-barreled revolver and held it up. I knew how to shoot, and the gun fit comfortably in my hand.

Before we moved into the new house, on a deserted beach in Crandon Park, my father took off the safety latch and pointed his handgun at a row of Coke cans he had lined up on a bent tree trunk in the distance. When he pulled the trigger, the first can disappeared in the blast. He let me try. I aimed carefully at the second can. The kick threw me back into my father who was standing behind me. The bullet missed the target. My hand shook.

"Aim more carefully," my father commanded, shoving me forward. "Spread your legs." I looked up at him, tall, tanned, and muscled, love for life shining in his eyes. I wanted to be like my father, fearless. I looked at the can and shut one eye, carefully measuring the distance. I breathed deeply and squeezed the trigger, keeping my arm steady and stiff, digging into the sand with my feet. The force from the gunpowder again threw me back, but not as far as before. This time the can flew into the air.

"Good shot," my father said. "Do it again."

I aimed at another can, bracing myself for the backward thrust. I pulled the trigger, and the can burst into pieces.

My father threw his head back and laughed, slapping his knee. I smiled, my heart expanding.

"You should have been a boy." I wondered why he said that, since I did everything I saw boys doing, but I felt dizzy and said nothing, wishing his pride in me would tie him closer to my mother. "If you're ever in trouble," he continued, "aim for the knees. You'll disable the attacker, not kill him."

Now, squatting on the floor of the closet, admiring the weapon, I rubbed a finger on the cold steel. I opened the cylinder and checked the bullets, one in each chamber. How could my father forget it in the box when he carried it with him everywhere he went? Had he purchased another gun for himself? I put it back into the pouch and slipped it under my blouse, as I had seen a neighbor kid shoplift soap from the corner drugstore, and crept quietly back to my room, making sure my mother, lying down, still slept. I placed the pouch underneath my bed, next to my diary, unzipped it, and moved it at just the right angle where I could reach it in a flash.

My Mother

My mother did her best to keep order, but she had little energy to notice much of what I did. She lay in bed all the time, staring at the ceiling and crying, the curtains drawn against the light. Sometimes she mopped the kitchen floor or vacuumed the living room carpet. I knew she was thinking about my father in Chicago or her relatives in Cuba. Sometimes she talked to visitors on the front porch, but when I went outside, nobody was there.

One night I heard my mother's voice, loud, agitated. I pulled out the gun, hid it under my pajama top, and rushed to her room. My mother stood by the window, peering out.

"Get out," she shouted into the darkness. "Go away. Stop bothering me!"

"Who is it?" I asked, and looked out with her, anxiously gripping the gun close to my beating heart. Not a leaf stirred. Only a dusty screen separated us from the backyard outside.

"They finally left," she said, turning away. "They came to poison me." She threw herself into bed and covered her head with the covers, not noticing the gun.

"Who wants to poison you?" Scared, confused, I strained to see shapes in the darkness, but nothing loomed out. Clutching the gun tighter, I grabbed the crank and closed the window as fast as I could. My mother did not answer.

Would I have the courage to shoot if someone tried to climb in through the window or broke down the door? What if the intruder tackled me to the ground before I had time to pull the trigger? Imagining the scene, I felt sweat on my face, back, stomach. I called to memory the images of the cans lined up on the tree trunk. I saw the cans explode. Then I saw a head explode into bloody pieces. Could I do that? No, I would aim for the knees, like my father said, keep him alive so he could go to prison.

I closed the blue satin curtain. I tiptoed past my mother's immobile body and returned to my room. I placed the gun under the bed, this time on top of the leather pouch. It had taken too long to pull it out of the case.

Margarita

I graduated from sixth grade on the honor roll, and with summer's heat and rain and mosquitoes, I ran free like a wild child. No father. No rules. Moving to this house just a year ago seemed another world. I went to sleep and woke up when I wanted. Neighborhood kids ran in and out of my house, banging doors and tracking in mud. We skated, biked, played freeze tag, and smoked cigarettes behind bushes.

At night we played cuarto obscuro, a hide-and-go-seek game in a dark room, usually a parent's bedroom because it was larger. One time, hiding under the bed, Marilyn brushed her lips against mine. The kiss felt dry, but it was hot and soft. Is that what it would feel like with a boy?

My record player shrieked with the Beatles' "I Want to Hold Your Hand" and a song by the Lovin' Spoonful about how summer made your neck feel gritty. We kept the front door open to catch a breeze; tall fans oscillated in the living room. My mother placed a small one on her dresser.

The Grosse Pointe Public Library, a block away on Seventh Street, offered a break from the heat. I read twenty-six books that summer and won first prize in a reading contest. The librarian posted my name and the titles of the books on pieces of colorful construction paper on a bulletin board. When I mentioned to my mother, her eyes shining with light that day, that I wanted to write books like the ones I read, she crossed the street and went to the admissions office of my school, enrolling me in a summer creative writing class. How did my mother know to do that?

The writing passion that would plague me throughout my life now had an outlet.

Humberto and Marta

Rosa's parents awoke before dawn to work ten hours each day in a shoe factory in the nearby city of Hialeah. Humberto operated a giant machine imprinting the soles, and Marta sewed on decorations at a small table. Humberto had been a political prisoner in Cuba. Someone said his time in El Morro, a medieval prison by the sea, made him go crazy. My mother wondered how anyone could be put behind bars just for spitting on the street in front of an army officer. Marta and Humberto never came out of their house when they were home, the blinds always drawn.

"How long do you have to go to college for?" I asked Rosa another time I caught her attention in the driveway.

"Four years. But it's worth it."

"I want to go to college, too."

"Yes, you must. Education will get you out of here and put money in your pocket. My father has neither; that's why he's going crazy. Now he's taken to roaming through the neighborhood all night long. He doesn't sleep anymore."

What?! Maybe it had been Humberto at my mother's window the other night.

"Does he go up to people's windows?"

"No. My mother watches him from the porch until he comes back. When he's in the house, all she does is watch him."

My Father

I closed the sliding glass door and sat down inside the phone booth at the corner drugstore. I clutched the receiver, dialed the operator, and asked for a collect call to Chicago. We didn't have a phone at home.

"Papi," I said when my father accepted the charges.

"¡Margarita! ¿Como estas?"

"Are we ever going to move to Chicago?"

"It's not a good time, yet. Your mother and I . . . well, I want to wait until. . . ."

"Papi, if we could be together, I would be so happy!"

"Did your mother tell you to say that?"

"No, and . . . and . . . we don't have much money left. Mi mamá says—"

"I knew it was your mother behind all this!"

I remembered my mother searching her purse for loose change, not complaining. Tears slid down my arm. "Am I going to see you again?"

"I'm leaving for Texas next week to work in a doctor's office," my father said. "It's a much better job than this one in the hospital. I'll arrange for you to visit as soon as I'm settled."

I placed the receiver back on its hook. I knew then that what I wanted most would never happen. My father had become a stranger. If my mother and I wanted to stay in the new house, we would have to figure out a way to pay the bills.

Margarita

Amid a fitful sleep at the peak of the summer's heat and

humidity, the night erupted in screams that threw fear and horror into the damp dark. The screams filtered through the branches of the guava trees in Mrs. Locklear's backyard next door and pierced the walls of my bedroom. My dreams split open, and I listened, thinking the shrieks were mine. I slipped my hand under the bed and gripped the gun. I put it under my pajama top and tiptoed out of my room. My mother hadn't stirred.

I looked out the front window. Mrs. Locklear stood on the sidewalk under a dazzling moon. "Is there a burglar?" I called out, not daring to open the door.

"No. The screams are coming from Rosa's house. It must be her father. I've already called the police. He didn't look good today at all."

I felt afraid, but the gun reassured me. I remembered my father saying safety meant having money in your pocket and a gun in your hand. He said his gun could blow anyone's head off from fifty yards away. But that was another gun, the one he had in Cuba. I wondered if this one was as powerful.

Mrs. White, the widow from the duplex, had moved in with Mrs. Locklear, and she too came out on the sidewalk, struggling toward wakefulness through a curtain of sedatives. Mrs. Locklear urged: "Go back to bed. Everything is all right." Mrs. White turned to go inside, and Mrs. Locklear motioned for me to join her. I slipped out the front door and closed it quietly behind me. Without a word, we edged closer to Rosa's house. Screams echoed through the neighborhood.

"I have a gun," I said.

"Good," Mrs. Locklear replied.

"Stop, stop!" I recognized the voice of Rosa's mother, Marta.

"No, Papi," Rosa cried out. "No, Papi."

The widower McCoy walked out of his house, face in the shadows, and stood motionless on the sidewalk. He looked at us in speechless despair, listening to his own silent screams. Mr. and Mrs. Kelly stood on their porch. Danny and Joey peeked from behind a curtain. Enrique and Concha opened their door and lingered in the doorway. Marilyn and Aurora stared at me through their bedroom window. Even Mrs. Smith ventured out, standing on the sidewalk with Mr. Smith next to her in the wheelchair, craning his neck to get a view.

"I have a gun," I repeated to Mrs. Locklear. "No one will hurt us."

I didn't know if she believed me, but the old woman put her hand on my shoulder and nodded as we moved behind the alcove of branches and leaves on one side of Rosa's yard. "We might need it," she said.

Mrs. Locklear was brave. Not me. My hands shook, but I knew I must pretend to have courage.

Through an open window, we saw Humberto sitting on a bed, holding a bloody knife in one hand and wiping away the tears dripping into his mouth with the other. We saw Marta, lying on the floor, groaning. Rosa, sobbing, trying to stop the bleeding with a towel, knelt at her side.

I drew a deep breath.

"Where are the police?" Mrs. Locklear whispered, frowning.

"Should I shoot Humberto? Maybe he's going to kill

Rosa!" I took the gun from under my pajama top and held it by my thigh. Just then, two police cars careened onto the front lawn; four officers jumped out, guns drawn, and rushed toward the house. The beams from their flashlights smashed through the cracks of the old wooden door.

"Miami police," one officer yelled.

I hid the gun behind my back. Humberto got up and opened the door, knife in hand. He charged past the officers and ran straight toward us. I raised the gun and spread my legs to keep my balance. I remembered the Coke cans on the log, and my father's advice about shooting an assailant in the knees. Humberto's legs were moving fast, but I was faster. I aimed carefully and pulled the trigger. The bullet shot forward, and my body jerked backwards, right into Mrs. Locklear. Almost at the same time, I heard another gunshot.

"Me cago en tu madre," Humberto yelled, falling less than a yard from our feet. I shoved the hot gun underneath my pajamas. Mrs. Locklear and I moved further back into the protection of the leaves.

Humberto writhed in pain, clutching his leg. Two officers ran to him, while the other two stood with guns pointed at the moaning man. One disengaged the knife from Humberto's hand and handcuffed him. Mrs. Locklear put her arm around me, and we stepped back even further into the leafy safety. The officers ignored us.

The wail of ambulances mixed with the laments from Rosa inside. Enrique crossed the street and joined us behind the branches.

"He must have gone crazy," Enrique said. "Who can accept living here after life in Cuba?"

Two paramedics lifted Humberto onto a stretcher and wheeled him into an ambulance; two others, working on the barely breathing Marta, wheeled her into the second ambulance. Rosa jumped in with her mother, and both ambulances screeched out of the yard and sped away, the patrol cars close behind.

The neighborhood lapsed into silence. I held the gun close to my body. Mr. McCoy walked back inside, his mouth twisted in anguish. The Smiths turned away. Mr. and Mrs. Kelly closed their door, and Danny and Joey ran to their rooms. Enrique combed his fingers through his hair, turned, and shuffled tiredly back to his house. Concha met him at the door; they embraced. Marilyn and Aurora waved from a window. I signaled "tomorrow we'll talk."

"Did I shoot Humberto?" I asked Mrs. Locklear.

"The police got him first."

"How do you know?"

"I don't. Let's hope that's what happened."

Mrs. Locklear and I walked toward our homes, hand in hand.

In my room, I placed the gun back under the bed. My mother still slept. I sensed the neighborhood settling down for what was left of the night. For one brief hour, the neighbors had taken part in their first common experience, united forever by this unforeseen violence, forgetting for the time their private pain, their public animosity. Would everyone be kinder now?

Those who dreamed of escaping exile, or were too old to dream, or wrestled with problems beyond their control, resumed the fitful sleep of discontent. Those who were in flux, neither here nor there, beginning their lives, stayed awake for a while longer, trying to figure it out. In a few weeks I would start seventh grade, maybe get a part-time job. My mother must get a job, too.

"I shot a man," I wrote in my diary, "and I will not need my father anymore. He's never coming back." The sweet smells of guava and mango trees and the bulbous pink flowers transplanted from La Habana stood still in the wet air, the tree leaves and flowers unruffled by the lack of an ocean breeze wished for so ardently, not only by the ones who lived in the past, but also by all of us who lived in the present, planned, and loved to go the beach because we knew what a cool blast of air could do.

Button Box

*The memories of childhood are like clear candles in
an acre of night.*

—Carson McCullers

Hidden in a floral-scented drawer in Tía Margot's walnut
armoire, a delightful treasure, buried in layers of imported
silk, linen, and cotton sateen, awaited discovery. Each Sunday I dug it out, a carved wooden box filled with buttons,
my imagination conjuring scenes of queens and princesses
decorating their robes with these very same disks and
spheres. Had these royals nervously fingered the cool marble, the reflecting glass, the intricately carved wood as they
waited to waltz in the court of the king?

In those prerevolutionary days of dictator Fulgencio
Batista, Tía Margot's house in Guanajay emanated the opu-
lence of Cuba's upper middle class, under siege by armed
Fidelista zealots hiding in the mountains. Just thirty minutes away from La Habana, this three-story tree-shaded

nineteenth-century town house looked like a Spanish castle. Medieval turrets decorated the roof on both sides. Coral tiles led the way from the narrow street to thick mahogany double doors with brass knockers in the shape of lions' heads. Thick walls, built from jagged rock blocks, cut the hand like a blade.

At the door with my parents on those sweltering Sundays, breezeless and cloudless, I was the first to cross the threshold into a dim foyer. Porous cream-colored limestone walls inside invited roaming fingers to rub shallow crevices. Marble slabs slipped under my feet as I trotted down a hallway and stepped onto the yielding fiber of a multicolored Persian rug in the sitting room. A circlet of lightbulbs in a dripping crystal chandelier pushed out the darkness.

Tía Margot, with smooth, alabaster complexion and humid black eyes, never forgot to warn me not to go into the courtyard because the dog was crazy.

"Está loco," she said in a whisper scented with café con leche.

My mother walked left and sat down with cousins, aunts, and uncles in overstuffed sofas and wing chairs. My father turned right, following Tío Lorenzo to an office whose gleaming white walls showcased imposing medical instruments. A long wooden examining table covered with a white sheet and outfitted with stirrups for gynecological examinations stood prominently in the center. Lorenzo eased into a delicately carved Louis XV chair next to a matching desk piled with charts and X-rays.

"Tío, how did Joseito make out after surgery?" My

father and Lorenzo, both physicians, spent hours in this room discussing patients, but I, impatient, rushed straight ahead, past the tantalizing smells of roast pork that the family would soon have to stand in long lines to get on the island, through the sitting room whose furniture would be sold to buy toothpaste and toilet paper, and into Tía Margot's elegant bedroom, where I yanked open the heavy drawer and reached inside, lifting the magical box out of the tangled mass of fabrics.

The scent of rose sachet flew into my face like butterflies. I climbed on a footstool, box in hand, and jumped on the bed covered with silvery satin sheets. Dislodging the top, I dug my fingers deep into its recesses, spilling the buttons on the sheet, imagining myself running through waves of buttons, rubbing them with the palm of my hand and letting them slip through my fingers to sort them into piles by color and shape. Much too soon, my father called from the living room: "Time to go!"

Reluctantly I put the box back into the stillness of the drawer. Taking advantage of the prolonged goodbyes at the door, I ignored Tía's warning, hurried into the greenery of the forbidden courtyard, and began the ritual of evading the dog. I heard him barking on the other side. Stumbling on slabs of stone leading to the old carriage house, I sped passed a white marble fountain holding up Cupid spurting water from his mouth. The smell of wilting roses filled the damp air. I inched along the narrow wall circling the courtyard and, reaching the opening toward the back, slinked inside the carriage house. The light fell in a slant through glass panes high above. Near the ceiling, a wide wooden ledge, once used to store bales of hay, swept all the way around.

From the other side, the dog sniffed my scent and sprinted toward me. I scurried up the unsteady ladder to the ledge, my heels just missing the dog's frenzied nipping. Once up near the rafters, I watched the crazy dog hurl himself at the ladder, steadily barking his frustration, eyes popping out of his head. He scratched furiously behind his ear; he licked between his legs. Turning, he streaked through the courtyard, a bullet of black and white, running wildly in a circle.

"Margarita, we're leaving," my mother called.

Making sure the dog was several feet away, I tore down the ladder and outran the raging dog back into the bedroom. "I'll be right there," I yelled, trying to quiet my breathing as I forced myself to walk slowly into the foyer to kiss Tía Margot and Tío Lorenzo goodbye, the last goodbye no one saw coming.

Decades later, still haunted by the box, and sick with longing for a time that had existed only briefly in my life but had taken on huge proportions in my mind, I tried to duplicate it at home in Miami. Red, blue, yellow, green plastic and glass buttons from dresses and blouses with labels like Liz Claiborne, Ann Taylor, Evan-Picone made their way into a wooden box my father had brought from Spain. This new box kept my memory intact; it served as a link to a past that had promised stability, warmth, and family love I couldn't find in America and a happiness, though imagined and built from photographs, I desired. In the box I saw the past as distant, but also close, a double image of color and light trapped within the shimmering buttons.

The nostalgia grew to unmanageable proportions, a burden every child carries from the lamentations of immigrant parents and the endless evenings of going through black-and-white photos filled with smiling ancestors in another land. One day, exasperated by an imagined memory that refused to abate, I planned a trip back to my homeland, intending to go in search of my old button box and affirm once and for all that my life in Miami could never be as good as it would have been back in 1950s Havana.

I wanted to see for myself, now as an adult, that wonderland in my parents' conversations, the place where I might have lived surrounded by the embrace of extended family instead of my chaotic Miami life filled with news about Colombian cocaine dealers, Nicaraguan contras, Haitian boat people, and Cuban rafters. I yearned to build a bridge linking my present self as a first-generation immigrant with that little girl who enjoyed simple pleasures on a lazy island that, while less than an hour away by plane, seemed to be on the other side of the globe.

It wouldn't be easy. For more than two decades the United States had shut the door to travel except to those visiting family members for humanitarian reasons, and Fidel Castro insisted that they had to have Cuban passports because they were still citizens of the nation he ruled.

Determined not to be thwarted, I secured a flight to the island through an agency called Marazul—enlisting the help of a friend who had a family member at death's door—and flew first to the Cuban Interests Section in

Washington, DC, to reclaim my Cuban citizenship which my parents had repudiated years ago.

Those at the window of the well-guarded office—shabbily dressed and speaking only Spanish—reluctantly stamped the passport. A few months later, with the newly acquired document in hand and a list of addresses and phone numbers in my bag, I boarded an early morning flight to La Habana, along with dozens of other Cuban exiles.

Each of us carted forty pounds of clothes, the maximum weight allowed by the Cuban government for destitute and ailing family members. Everyone but me wore two or three skirts or pants, one on top of the other, and several belts and sweaters to circumvent the weight limit. The flight across the Straits of Florida was so short that no one in the stuffy cabin had time to soak the clothes with sweat.

When I stepped onto Cuban soil, and the still summer morning heavy with humidity touched me with its heat, I felt a wide gulf between my fellow passengers and me. I was an outsider and, unlike them, had embarked on this trip to fulfill a desire brought on by thinking too much about my identity. I didn't have sick or needy relatives clamoring for clothes and medicine. Everyone on that flight seemed to belong to the island, as if they had never left.

I hurried to a bus waiting to take our group into the city and glanced at tall billboards proclaiming a workers' state with slogans like "Unidos Venceremos," united we shall overcome. On the road, rattling cars from the 1950s, repaired endlessly, raced past. At the drop-off point I hailed a cab to my first stop, the apartment of my Miami friend's aunt, and delivered the forty pounds of clothes; I planned on giving cash to Tía Margot.

The song "Amadeus" hurtled from a dilapidated boom box and bounced off the walls of the Spanish colonial tenement building where I spent the night. After a tormented sleep, I awoke to the early morning shouts of a truck driver bringing fresh water to the area. The residents ran out from their homes in various stages of dress lugging pails to capture the fresh clear liquid flowing from the truck.

"He only comes once a week," my friend's aunt said.

The unfamiliar sights and sounds of La Vieja Habana—the old colonial section of the city—swirled around me as I dressed quickly and drank a bitter, watery café con leche in the cramped room that served as living room, bedroom, and dining room for four people. The heat pressed in, unrelieved by the air conditioning that seemed like a right in Miami. Outside, narrow cobblestoned streets separated solid walls of buildings. Laundry hung from windows to dry. Running everywhere, children shouted, and adults screamed back. Everyday speech spilled out of open doorways, ready to be shared with anyone. I could have been living here, too, I thought; this could have been my life.

The aunt's husband drove me to an old rental car lot where, promising my new friends that I would return to their apartment after visiting my great-aunt and great-uncle, I rented a Soviet-made Lada and began the anxiously awaited thirty-mile drive to Guanajay, glancing every so often at my mother's written directions on a sheet of paper fluttering on the passenger seat.

My hands trembled on the wheel as I turned down a narrow street and parked outside the old townhouse of my childhood. The memory crumbled, stopping me from running to the door. A dingy yellow paint covered walls scuffed with unidentifiable black marks, the paint torn off in chunks in many places, the tiled walkway chipped, worn down. As with all returns, everything appeared smaller.

The turrets still stood high above me, imposing, but gray now with cracks in the glass windows. It occurred to me that I could turn around and drive off. No one knew I was coming. Instead I propelled myself forward. The brass lion's-head knockers were missing. I rapped on the thick door with my knuckles. Minutes passed. The door opened a crack. I introduced myself to a shadow standing just inside.

"Ay, ¿eres tu? ¿La hija de Carmencita?" Tía Margot exclaimed, remembering me as my mother's daughter. She shoved open the door and stared into my face, unbelieving. She thought nothing of my unexpected visit. Throughout the years, relatives of neighbors did the same without warning, she said.

"It takes months for a letter to arrive," Margot said. "And it's almost impossible to get a call through on the phone lines, so we never know who will be visiting."

Tío Lorenzo remained silent at her side but smiling. A stroke had stolen his power of speech. His step was halting as he turned to walk me down the hall to the sitting room.

"You look just like your mother," Margot told me.

White-haired, stooped, Margot and Lorenzo at eighty and eighty-two had the same strong, distinctive features

I remembered. Their wrinkled faces expressed a range of emotions, and their high spirits flew from their eyes.

As we walked, I noticed the darkness. No lightbulbs sparkled in the chandelier. Rust coated the brass fixtures on smudged walls. The once-smooth marble floors felt uneven, and the Persian rug was worn thin.

In the sitting room, a young woman held two toddlers on her lap on the couch, now covered with torn towels. The children, noses and mouths smudged with food, looked scared.

"This is Marlene, Enriquito's daughter," Margot said, "and these are my great-grandchildren, Patricia and José." Enriquito, Margot's son and my mother's cousin, had introduced my parents while he and my father studied at the University of Havana. Enriquito now lived on the other side of the island, and no one talked about him.

His daughter, slender with heavy dark hair pulled to the side, smiled the warm but timid smile of my mother's family. Then I looked into the eyes of the man seated next to her: Marlene's husband, Pablo. This young man worked in the fields all day and came home each night to the luxury of the beloved nineteenth-century castle of my childhood.

"Es comunista," my great-aunt later whispered. Because of him, we spoke in whispers in the kitchen. "Don't say anything against Fidel," she warned.

No more the loud laughter of my childhood or the complex language of Tío Lorenzo's medical world. This time, we made small talk about family members in Miami and those who had decided to stay in Cuba.

Pablo, sullen, stared at me, an intruder into my past, and I met his gaze with defiance. Burnt skin covered the bulges of his arms. His black hair gleamed with grease. I imagined him fingering the buttons, in wonderment at the unfamiliar sensation. Would he understand the days of magic in the bedroom and the courtyard, the time before Castro descended from the Sierra Maestra and triumphantly claimed La Habana?

"I'm going to the American store tomorrow," I said.

Pablo took out several American bills, black market dollars, from his pocket and handed them to me. "Can you buy us some clothes?" He wanted running shoes and jeans. The store, or "diplo-tienda," was banned to Cubans, but I, an exile, could shop there with dollars and deliver the merchandise to my relatives without repercussions.

"Sí, cómo no." Of course.

By now I was impatient with the small talk and anxious to go in search of the box. I made my move.

"May I use the bathroom, please?"

"Por supuesto, hija," my great-aunt answered. Certainly.

I walked out of the sitting room and into the hallway adjoining the bedrooms. I remembered that the first one was Tía Margot's. I opened the door and stepped inside, entering the time and space of 1958. There, all around, sprang up the textured, freshly painted limestone walls, the silver satin bedsheets, and the lacquered walnut armoire. I dug into a drawer. Was it this one? No. Another drawer. Again, no. Then, yes. Here it was.

The fine fabrics, shreds now, still wrapped themselves

protectively around the box. I pulled it out and opened the lid. Colored buttons spilled on the floor and onto my feet. They loomed large as balloons and floated around me, bouncing against walls and onto my skin, the four-poster bed, the embroidered linens. The memories shut me away from the revolutionary government outside and I became little Margarita again, laughing joyfully and forgetful of the time.

With box in hand, I made my way out of the bedroom and tiptoed into the forbidden courtyard. I heard the barks of the dog and felt the fear-sparked adrenaline. I heard my father arguing with Tío Lorenzo in the medical office and my mother and her aunt laughing on the couch. I peeked around the door and mounted the rickety ladder. There I was, once again hiding in the carriage house, enjoying the illicit view of the courtyard, looking down at the dog. Holding on to the box with one hand, I reached inside with the other. I examined each piece of glass, marble, metal, and wood. It must have been hours before I finished looking at each button.

Unaware of the time, I climbed down and slipped into the bedroom. I placed the box back in the drawer and covered it with the rumpled fabrics. It belonged here in this world, intact in reality and in memory, just as part of me would belong always on this island. I realized that, back in Miami, while I had grown into a different person than the one that may have existed here, I would never shed the longing for this world, the world of our stories, and, like every immigrant, I would never stop mourning its loss.

I shut the drawer, dropped my head into my hands,

and waited for the pain to subside. I turned to go back to the sitting room and met the smiling, tearing eyes of Tía Margot. She stood at the doorway, holding a creased black-and-white photo of me and the crazy dog. I reached out to take it and fell into her hug. This castle held the last of my family on the island. They would cease to exist at some moment in time, but, like the crazy dog and the button box, would remain unchanged inside my memories.

Where Do You Go, My Lovely?

Susana knew Dan was watching from the limousine as she flung back her wrist, bracelets glowing in the light of the hotel's outdoor lamps, and brought it forward with a decided motion. The tropical night sky of South Florida broke open with lightning, and Susana hit her mark: Dean Buonfiglio's jaw. The bone-cracking sound bounced unimpeded through the beachside buzzing. Someone gasped.

"Let me go," Susana yelled when the dean's hand closed on her forearm. Fifteen gold bangles desperately tried to escape the confines of her wrist.

Moments before, she had come out of the hotel bathroom and, descending the stairs to the waiting limo, locking blacklined eyes with Dan, tripped on the long skirt of the prom gown she had designed with such care, such concentration. The flowing material, which her father had imported from France, wrapped itself in soft emerald-green folds around her ankles. She stumbled and gripped the handrail for balance just as the dean rushed to her side. Susana had to stop him from touching her before things got out of control inside her head, but the blow failed to fend him off.

Dean Buonfiglio led her—maybe with just a slight shove—down the remaining stairs. Susana, squirming, frowning, mouth twisted, heard the waves slap the shore across the street from the Fort Lauderdale Marina Hotel. If only she could run to the water's edge and cool her feet, submerge her head in the sea froth, design sand castles as she used to do as a child, she could forget about her low SAT scores and the pile of rejection letters from every university to which she had applied. Maybe she could find the courage to break up with Dan, to leave home, to enroll at the Art Institute downtown, to go, go, go, and never look back.

She turned her head toward the beach as the dean dragged her forward. How could she slip out of his iron clasp? Above, stars shivered in the black sky, and Susana closed her eyes against the cruel, harsh reality of her disappointing life.

Behind closed lids, images of her parents' angry faces crept into her chemically befuddled brain. She heard her father shout, "We came from Cuba without a penny, we worked like animals to make something of ourselves, and now you throw it all away!" Then her mother's scream: "I've done everything to give you the advantages I never had!" The roots of Susana's Cuban family were planted only recently in the USA, but her parents' relentless striving for success had already made them rich. Their daughter refused, or was unable, to live up to the promise her parents had made when she was born in a country that was not theirs: "This child is going to Harvard." Not Harvard, not anywhere, Susana voiced inside her head. I'm a failure, total failure. That unshakable feeling had made her last months of high school an agonizing ordeal, relieved only by a blurry vision of running away. The moon played hide-and-seek behind the clouds, and the wind announced rain.

"You're going to be expelled," the dean said, as he pushed her down into the front passenger seat of his car.

Susana shrugged.

Dan leaned out the window as far as he dared from his seat in the limo. He could see Susana's slack facial muscles and unfocused gaze. But he caught the quick clarity-filled glance she shot him before her head disappeared into the dean's car; it said, "This is the real me. Not the passive, sweet girl everyone likes. I'm sick of you, and I'm sick of following rules." His two buddies and their dates held flasks half-filled with cheap wine just out of sight, eyes nervously darting from Dan to Susana outside.

"She's leaving me," he muttered. He had sensed her utter boredom with him weeks ago. "But I'm leaving first cuz I got a scholarship outta here."

He slumped back into the supple leather of his seat. A running back on the football team at Immaculate Conception High School, Dan felt his muscles push against the tight-fitting tux. He had been accepted at Auburn University, and although the school had a lenient 80 percent acceptance rate, it was good enough for him, the great-great-grandson of Italian immigrants and the first in his family to go to college. He couldn't let Susana's rage interfere with his future.

He rubbed his face, olive-tinged with a crooked Roman nose broken twice on the football field, slicked-back black hair coming loose from the heavy gel used to control it. He closed his eyes and loosened his bowtie. He'd deny everything.

The night had begun innocently enough. Dan pinned an orchid corsage on Susana's dress just below her shoulder soon after getting to her house. Susana's parents, grandparents, aunts, uncles, and cousins jostled for space in the living room, trying to get the best shot of the couple, shouting to each other, "If only María, or Juan, or José in Cuba could see us now!" The teenagers' gleaming teeth competed with the flash of Nikons and Canons, recording prom night history forever. On one of Susana's wrists, fifteen bangles kept up with her every move; on the other, a charm bracelet, sparkling like the flame of a cigarette lighter, told its story. One charm in the shape of a stop sign proclaimed, "I will never stop loving you." Another, encrusted with rubies and emeralds, bore the shape of a birthday cake with a 15 in the middle and bumped into one of the Eiffel Tower. A fourth, a tiny ring holding a garnet chip, once had encircled her grandfather's finger as a toddler in La Habana, a coddled upper-class boy destined for greatness before the Marxist-Leninist takeover of the island.

Susana lived in a Miami neighborhood of first- and second-generation Cuban Americans who owned the American Dream. Her gated community boasted million-dollar houses with winding staircases and foyers displaying paintings by the Old Masters. French or Chinese antique tables bought in Europe for the price of a Mercedes lined the walls. Crystal chandeliers dripped toward marble floors. Outside, trimmed hedges separated each house from the next, purple bougainvillea guarded second-floor windowsills, kidney-shaped pools sparkled in the sun, and BMWs, Bentleys, or Jaguars sat under shady palms in circular driveways.

The business executives, lawyers, and doctors who lived here had watched their parents struggle with the English language in the 1960s, Susana's grandfather among them, and work long hours in factories by day to rebuild professional careers by night, sometimes studying until dawn for foreign board exams and revalidation licenses. They listened as Mami and Papi vowed to regain what they had lost when they fled their communist island nation with only a few hundred dollars sewn inside their clothes. They had absorbed the work ethic—and the pride in their culture—and been successful. They wanted their children to climb to the top of the status ladder just as they had. While the grandparents spent their last years relaxing in the in-law quarters, the new generation, Susana's, prepared to leave home for college. These teens had been groomed by English, math, music, and French tutors, and a string of SAT instructors. Everything that money could buy to launch their success had been their birthright. Some had been accepted at Harvard, Duke, Stanford. Others at the University of California, Virginia, North Carolina. No one was staying home.

The dream had never been Susana's. She didn't want to go away to college. Yes, she excelled in art, and that talent, her mother insisted, would make her rich and famous if only she could channel it into architecture. To Susana, symbols of affluence were simply part of an unchanging, familiar landscape. She didn't have an interest in anything but sketching and painting. She loved the feel of grainy, chalky charcoal between her fingers and obsessively created portraits of friends, teachers, parents, brothers, grandparents, and neighbors. She painted in watercolors: her school, house, pool, and gardens. She tried acrylic, her canvases—echoes of Matisse, Picasso, Chagall—taking up every inch of her bedroom walls.

To her classmates Susana appeared surreal, evanescent, not quite a hermit but a loner, someone who listened while others talked and who never, ever, unlike the other girls, flaunted her formidable beauty. Inside, deep within, lived another person, passionate, willful, vengeful. One who, when no one was looking, attacked her nails with her teeth until they bled, trying to figure out how she could do what she wanted against the resolute wills of her parents. To appease them, she had applied to the California College of the Arts, the Fashion Institute in New York, the Savannah College of Art and Design, and the Pratt Institute, all the while only wanting to take classes at the art school downtown. Her mother, Marisol, shook her head. There's no money in art, she said. But there is in architecture, at least more than in art. And we have many neighbors who will want a bigger mansion and will hire you! When Susana's rejection letters started to trickle in, Marisol buried her face in her hands and sat on the couch all night.

Maybe she'll marry a doctor, said her father, Leo, fixing himself a rum and Coke. Tonight, prom night, signaling high school graduation, a milestone in Susana's path to success, no one would mention college.

"Have fun!" Leo and Marisol shouted, shoving aside their daughter's future for the time being. The hordes of relatives pressed forward on the flagstone walkway. Curious neighbors across the street came out as the black limo stretched out of the driveway and sped away, windows so darkly tinted the vehicle looked like a moving coffin. Marisol wiped away a tear. Leo wrapped his arm around her shoulders. They walked back to the house and into the embrace of their festive family. As a defense attorney, Leo had millions in the bank. He wouldn't let his daughter starve, but her mother had different ideas. She wanted Susana to be somebody, to be respected socially and professionally like she was, as the president of the League Against Cancer and owner of a thriving public relations firm. She would not give up on her daughter. This is just a temporary setback, she declared.

The limo had not gone more than a mile before Susana and Dan tipped flasks filled with wine to their lips; their companions, two other couples, did the same. The tinted windows offered anonymity, and they relaxed in the air-conditioned darkness. Dan brought out the white powder. Susana paused, then leaned forward. Why not? Just one time wouldn't hurt. And if it did, she didn't care. Tonight she would be free of home pressure and do what she wanted. Then she would make her move. The couples laughed and joked. The Fort Lauderdale Intracoastal Waterway sped by.

"Love you, baby," Dan said, and held Susana's hand. A strand of highlighted hair poked out of Susana's carefully twisted chignon. Her brown eyes tilted downward at the corners when she laughed, and her full lips revealed a tiny chip on her right front tooth. Her form-fitting dress displayed a sinuous figure: two straps of satin curled around her breasts to lock onto the waistband in the back. She rested her eyes on Dan and felt the urge to sketch him, but she did not say "Love you" back.

Dan's tux offered a glimpse of a Christmas-red vest just below a bow tie of the same color. The white of his freshly starched shirt spread like rice across his broad chest. His jaw, square as a box, moved in a chewing motion, and he twitched the muscle next to his ears when he frowned. He reached over and tucked Susana's body closer into his. She squirmed free. They stared out the window, watching the cars flow by on this night of nights, unable to formulate a thought they could later remember as the effects of cocaine and alcohol spread into the synapses of the brain.

Dan, like Susana, was not a brilliant student. He had barely made the grades to qualify for the football scholarship. What mattered most to him was rushing through an opposing line with the ball close to his heart, running toward the glory and the power of making a touchdown. Without this college opportunity, he might have to work at his parents' greasy spoon for the rest of his life. He hated going there to take pizza and spaghetti orders after football practice, but he needed the cash and withstood the sickening smell of tomato sauce and stale beer.

Susana tipped her head back on Dan's shoulder in a

spell of dizziness. "Everything will change after tonight," she said.

"How so?" Dan asked.

She shook her head. The line of cocaine they had snorted blasted through her brain. Her French-manicured acrylic nails tapped the armrest to the music from the CD player, "Forever Young" by Rod Stewart. Dan's two friends ignored them, lost in kissing their girlfriends.

"My mother wants me to remember this day forever," Susana continued. "She says nothing will be the same afterwards because I have to get serious about my future, which means making money. But really. I don't care about the future. I want to be an artist, that's all."

"Uh-huh," Dan mumbled, moving to kiss her fleeting lips.

"What future will I have if they won't let me paint?"

"Don't know."

"I'm going to the art school downtown no matter what my parents say. It's my life. I can do what I want with it."

The limo slid up to the hotel. Dan, Susana, and their friends emerged dazed from the polished vehicle. Loud music reached them as they ascended the staircase to the grand ballroom. Teacher chaperones greeted them and ushered them to their places at a banquet table set with crystal goblets and rows of silver forks, knives, and spoons. Waiters with trays crammed with shrimp cocktails and goat cheese salads gyrated around the room, beginning to serve. The three couples sat down to quench thirst and quell hunger.

"What are we doing after prom?" Dan spoke into Susana's ear.

"Anything but go home."

"My aunt's gone for the weekend. I have a key."

"Uff."

After a while Susana excused herself from the table, found the bathroom, and entered one of the stalls. Taking out the flask that Dan had slipped into her purse, she lifted it to her lips and swallowed. She flushed the toilet and walked out to join Dan on the dance floor now packed with couples. As she danced, she thought about the upcoming summer, working in her father's law firm for extra cash. Maybe she could save the money to move out. She could apply for a student loan for Art Institute tuition. She thought of her stacks of sketchbooks, her paintings on the wall. Could she become an artist? How would she go about it?

Dean Buonfiglio reached over and snapped the seat belt around Susana, who glared at him from half-closed eyes. He turned the key in the ignition, and the car lunged out of the parking lot. Susana turned to the window and sighed. "My parents can't be more upset anyway," she said. "What's one more disappointment? I don't care."

The dean, not unsympathetic, didn't answer. His eyes slid over Susana's figure. He was fifty-five years old and married for too long, but he couldn't let desire get in the way of his job. Rain smacked the windshield as he pulled up to her house. The dean hurried Susana up the broad front steps under the covered entrance, dry from the the downpour. When Marisol opened the door, she glanced at her daughter's eyes and shouted: "I'm going to get Dan arrested for corrupting a minor! I know it's all his fault that you are drunk." The dean opened his mouth to speak, but she cut him off. "I want him expelled. He made her intoxicated."

"She's the one getting expelled," the dean slipped in. "She punched me!"

Susana stopped listening to her mother's shrieks. She tiptoed up to her room, but not before she heard Leo hurl something at the Louis XV mirror in the living room.

On Monday afternoon, Dan and his parents sat in the principal's office waiting for the dean. Gray-haired Sister Mary, principal at Immaculate Conception for two decades, had soothed many parents and students in her long career. These families paid a lot of money for the privilege of a Catholic education at her school, and they gave generous donations besides. Long childhood years of helping her family raise funds for the Irish American Army battling for the end of British rule in Northern Ireland had molded her tough demeanor. Crooked teeth streaked with yellow indicated a life of poverty. The dean, elegantly dressed in a three-piece suit and silk tie, sat in the next office talking to Susana's mother on the phone. He hung up and walked in, shaking his head. His eyes, under bushy brows, bore into Dan.

"This is pretty serious. You and Susana were drinking and doing coke in the limo and the hotel bathroom. Susana's parents say you brought the drugs and alcohol, and you are responsible for her behavior. They want you expelled from school."

"His friends brought the drugs," Dan's mother yelled, slumping back in her chair. "It wasn't Danny!"

"My son did not force Susana into taking drugs," his father said with eyes fixed on the wall clock, one fist in the palm of his hand.

"Dean, Susana brought the drugs and alcohol in her purse," Dan defended himself. "No one else in the limo took anything but her. She said she wanted this to be a night to remember. She insisted. I knew it was wrong. It was not my fault. I couldn't control her."

"Son, you have a week left before you graduate. You're going away to college, right?"

Dan nodded and looked down at his folded hands.

"Is this the way you want everyone to remember you?"

Coming out of her silence, Sister Mary struck a deal.

Rain beat on Susana's umbrella as she avoided puddles in the empty parking lot of the school. Friday, last day of class, and she had the week's assignments to hand in. After prom, she had not gone back, but she had not been expelled. Dan hadn't either. Sister Mary had made the decision that, in exchange, neither would participate in graduation ceremonies on Saturday to avoid bad publicity. She managed to convince both sets of parents to agree.

Susana stepped into a passageway to shake the water from her umbrella and spied her art teacher on the way to the weekly faculty meeting. She turned away and walked in a different direction to the counselor's office.

Three doors down in the media center, teachers took their seats, whispers fleshing out the details of the prom story. Sister Mary called the meeting to order and led the group in prayer. After the blessing, she faced the faculty. She unfolded a letter from an envelope and read: "My daughter has become the laughingstock of the school. Her friends tell her that teachers talk about her in the classroom; students whisper in the hallways. A young girl who was always happy now can't even go out in public." Sister Mary folded the letter back into the envelope. The teachers lowered their eyes.

Down the hall, Susana placed the folder with her completed assignments on the counter. "You'll get your diploma in the mail," the counselor said in a cheery tone. "Don't feel discouraged. One day, this will just be a story to tell your children."

Susana nodded and walked back in the rain to her car. I'm going to do things my way now, she thought. On Monday, I'm going to the art school in Miami and registering for classes, even if I pay for them myself.

She had no phone or computer, so she had to register in person. When her mother took the devices away, she laughed.

That evening, Dan hurriedly threw clothes into his suitcase for his predawn flight the next day. Sister Mary had not allowed him to stay home from school that last week. His father called it "getting off easy" and phoned Auburn University officials to arrange for Dan to go up early as an assistant residence manager. The college offered summer classes to gifted high school students, and the dorm needed an extra supervisor who could do a little football coaching on the side. "I'm not coming home for Thanksgiving or Christmas," he said at the airport. "I want everyone to forget everything that happened before I come back. Maybe you can visit me instead."

"That's probably best," his father answered. His mother nodded.

Flags and Rafts

A month of lying on a heating pad with a back sprain cost Adela a boyfriend and two paychecks, but it gave her time to watch the Coast Guard rescues on the news. Five years of Cuba's período especial, a severe economic crisis, had pushed hundreds—no, thousands—of balseros, or rafters, into the sea, paddling their way from the seventeenth-century port of Cojímar to Miami.

The camera caught the gaunt faces of men, women, and children balancing themselves on rafts made from empty oil drums, inner tubes, and wooden planks in the rough seas of the Straits of Florida, stretching out arms to officers who hauled them aboard their cutters. She looked closely at each, searching for familiar faces. What if he had perished at sea? What if he had slipped into the country and she didn't know it? That old love left behind decades ago always lurked near, never forgotten.

During Adela's month in bed, her new boyfriend reevaluated their relationship, and as she shifted on the hard mattress under the daze of OxyContin, she heard the

Texan man she'd met on a dating site say he was return-
ing to his family in San Antonio. Today, over him at last,
she was going back to work. One foot in front of the other,
Adela willed herself to walk the few blocks to her job at the
American Flag Company, a small struggling factory just
south of the bridge spanning the brown, polluted Miami
River, that highway of illegal entry for cocaine, marijuana,
and Haitian refugees. This was what old age felt like: hob-
bling along, pausing for breath. As usual, she arrived first
at work.

Raimundo dragged his right leg behind him, leaving a long,
thin trail in the dirt as he groped his way in the darkness
to the waiting pickup truck. The engine gurgled as if trying to clear the congestion of a bad cold. He climbed into
the passenger seat, reached down, and lifted his leg inside.
Cousin Paquito backed out of the narrow Habana Vieja
alleyway and steered the heavy vehicle east to the narrow
coastal road that led to the port of Cojímar, a dozen miles
away, where once Ernest Hemingway docked his famous
boat, the *Pilar*. Few in Cuba cared about that piece of trivia,
least of all Paquito's two nephews, Tommy and Beto, muscled and tanned thirtysomethings who sat silently in the
back, exhausted from wrestling the makeshift raft out of
the apartment and into the truck. All four men wore old
cutoff jeans and frayed T-shirts, as if headed to a fishing
expedition.

   But that August of 1994, fishing was the last thing on
their minds. The island had slid into the ultimate misery,
a wave of famine, and they were leaving. Since the Soviet

Union, now Russia, had pulled out and gone home, Cubans had resorted to eating anything they could find. In the Habana zoo, the peacocks, the buffalo, and even the rheas disappeared, as well as the cats that roamed the streets.

In this predawn morning, Raimundo knew he had made the right decision, and not because he didn't have enough to eat. He had grown up with the revolution Fidel had orchestrated back in 1959, daring to dream that Cubans of the future would enjoy true social and economic freedom. He worked tirelessly alongside Castro's top echelon, selflessly, to transform the island into a socialist state, a Cuba for Cubans.

When he paused to look around, he saw that, instead, the system had changed into a repressive regime far worse than any that Castro's predecessor, the dictator Fulgencio Batista, could have designed in the forties and fifties. Raimundo sat in his office and wept, realizing that his efforts to throw out the mafia and greedy American corporations had not amounted to much. In the darkness, bouncing on the bumpy roads in his cousin's truck just before the sun announced a new day, he gripped the sides of the seat and stared straight ahead.

Adela turned the rusted key and shoved open the heavy door. The flag factory's musty, cool interior embraced her. She leaned against the wall, readjusting the stiff back support soaked in sweat, closing her eyes against the pain. Tall and slim, as beauty is defined in the world, she pushed aside lustrous, only lightly gray-streaked hair for which she always thanked a secret African ancestor. Today her gaze did not radiate fun from heavily lashed almost-black eyes. Nor did a smile flash simultaneously with a gentle chuckle. She tried to lift her mood and told herself: I'm only sixty-two and still fresh and vibrant, and just maybe, as soon as my back heals, I can attract another lover.

She walked over to the old Singer sewing machine, brand new when she first went to work for American Flag for ninety dollars a week thirty years ago. The factory had not changed much, just three seamstresses in the space of a large living room with infrequent visits from the owner who had made her the unofficial supervisor and entrusted her with the key. She settled into the unyielding steel chair, moved the cushion around to support her back, and pushed the On button. She took up a red and a white strip of canvas from a stack, aligned them under the presser foot of the sewing machine, and reached with her toes for the pedal.

The flying needle pecked out a whirring rhythm between the narrow steel bars of the presser foot, breaking the silence that would last until her two coworkers traipsed to their chairs sometime in the next hour She admired the jagged trail of thread that joined the pieces. Yes, this was much easier than stitching, by hand, the long ropes of pearls or webs of rhinestones on ball gowns when she lived in La Habana.

The old 1950s truck rattled over potholes, threatening to blow a tire as it climbed out of a deep crevice in the road. Raimundo turned his face to the sea, an expanse of black with white-capped waves below, slamming against craggy rocks.

Years ago, after stowing his trousers and shirt behind a bush, he'd dive into the blue-green ocean, feeling the water slip along his body like fingers as he swam down to touch the sand. Back then, hope and energy mingled to keep him loyal to Fidel's government. Emerging from the sea, he'd gazed on the beloved hills and valleys and—in the sunlight—he thought of God. Some years after that, he couldn't tell exactly when, he stopped believing.

In the predawn, a thin layer of fog floated above the same landscape, and the bohíos, the huts with grass-thatched roofs, peeked through. "Beautiful," he said, and turned to stare at the roadway. He gripped the seat firmly, trying to lessen the bouncing.

At sixty-eight, he wore a patchy beard on a tanned face. Dark pouches circled sunken eyes. His hair, thin and wispy at the crown, grew full and white at the temples. Who would believe he had been handsome? At least he kept his muscles toned with daily push-ups on the floor of his small apartment in a crumbling colonial building. Sometimes, lost in the exercise, he didn't hear the water truck outside, but he didn't mind, even if it meant going without washing for a week. He hated to join the shouting neighbors shoving with their pails for water, standing in yet another line for life's bare necessities.

Quietly he had survived ten years of ostracism after he denounced the government from the stoop of his apartment building. He endured through a daily exaltation of the will and the wise stewardship of his resources, stockpiling bars of soap, shaving cream, blocks of cheese, even bottles of wine that Canadian and Australian tourists slipped him as he guided them on historical walks through the city.

Six months before, he'd had no choice but to quit his job as a tour guide. A mild stroke had paralyzed his right foot, making it difficult to walk. Then hunger had forced Paquito, a fiftysomething cousin, and his two nephews to come from the countryside to live with him. He had welcomed the company and the help in acquiring provisions. The three men resorted to stealing and working in the underground market; the nephews dabbled in prostitution for a gallon of gas, a loaf of bread, and kept the household running.

"We have to get out of here," Paquito finally said. He and his nephews began hauling in inner tubes, stolen rope, and salvaged pieces of canvas at all hours of the night. Soon they had enough material to start constructing a raft in the middle of the room.

"I can't bear the corruption and oppression anymore," Raimundo told his relatives. Today, August 15, 1994, he would dare to live again.

Before long, two young women—recent Cuban rafters themselves—banged open the door and made their way to sewing machines adjoining Adela's. They kept up a lively chatter about dating, dancing at clubs, and taking English classes at the local high school. Adela nodded in their direction. The women ignored her although they knew she kept an eye on the quality of their work. No love lost between the newly arrived and those who had fled decades ago; class and politics formed an unscalable wall between them in the Cuban community.

Around Adela on the factory walls, shelves sagged under the weight of red, white, and blue fabric rolls. She kept up a steady rhythm on her sewing machine without taking a break until lunchtime. Then she shuffled to the small black-and-white TV suspended on the wall with steel brackets and tuned in to NewsCenter 7 at Noon, the portal to events she, in her humdrum life, could almost touch, especially the news about her homeland.

This summer, Cuban rafters were making international news, washing up on shore,   dying on the high seas, being rescued by the Coast Guard in record numbers. Adela peered into the TV screen. As the cameras zoomed in on the sun-poisoned, dehydrated, and blistered refugees, she never failed to carefully search each face for friends and relatives and, especially, for him. Had he regretted his decision to stay behind?

"Heroism of weakness," Raimundo called the steady flow of rafters bound for US shores. His decision now made him a hero too, along with dozens of asylum seekers recently killed by Cuban officials in a series of boat hijackings. One of the boats, a ferry, ran out of gas at sea. When Cuban officials arrested the pilot, a riot erupted in La Habana, police clubbing demonstrators. In the chaos, a rumor circulated that a flotilla of boats was on its way to pick up people seeking to leave. Many rushed to the shore, peering out into the empty horizon, hoping for another boatlift like the one in 1980, when 125,000 escaped aboard boats that came to pick them up from Miami. But this time Cubans waited in vain.

Finally, Fidel demanded that the United States intercept the balseros and send them back. Not getting the response he wanted, he opened the ports to anyone who wanted to leave. As thousands raced to construct makeshift vessels, Paquito and Raimundo, along with other visionaries, had already finished theirs.

"To jump in the water is to sell our lives," Raimundo said, his eyes fixed on the old sputtering vehicle ahead on the dark coastal highway to Cojímar. "This is an adventure without end." Paquito didn't answer, full attention on the road. Sleep had claimed Tommy and Beto in the backseat.

The news anchor said that only one out of four Cubans on rafts arrived alive in South Florida. The video rolled, and Adela, gripping the table's edge, watched a group of anti-Castro Cubans calling themselves Hermanos al Rescate—Brothers to the Rescue—soar through the air in small propeller planes, spotting their drowning countrymen amid wall-high waves and hungry sharks and notifying the Coast Guard to rescue the immigrants. The news said that President Clinton was negotiating a "dry foot, wet foot" immigration policy with Cuba: rafters caught at sea would be returned to the island. Anyone who made it past the Coast Guard and set foot on dry land could stay. The plan would go into effect in a few weeks. Could he be one of the lucky ones? If he lived, could they revive their love? They were old now, but still in time to start over.

When the men reached the port of Cojímar, the darkness

surrendered to the first feeble rays of sun. Raimundo looked at the hundreds of men, women, and children already there, most dressed in bathing suits or shorts and ragged tank tops or T-shirts. One woman clad in white robes, with a white turban tightly wound around her head, strode back and forth on the rocky shore, babbling to the heavens.

There, on the wet, hard sand, hopeful men and women tied and hammered together wood, inner tubes, canvas strips, empty oil drums. Some strung plastic bottles filled with water on a rope, securing them to the edges of the rafts, and crammed a few loaves of bread into plastic bags before throwing themselves into the sea. Others pulled up in trucks whose eager passengers lifted out sophisticated, well-constructed rafts—many with motors—and ran toward the shore as if their burden were weightless.

Paquito stopped the pickup several yards from the water's edge. Raimundo pushed open the door, eased his immobile leg out, and leaned on the other. Shouts from the seashore awakened Tommy and Beto. They jumped out, suddenly alert, ran to the back of the truck, and pulled out their homemade raft, letting it slide to the ground. The two jacked up the rickety vehicle, one side and then the other, removed the wheels, and excised the four inner tubes. Pumping them back up, they tied them to the underside of the six they had already, lashed together with ropes and wrapped neatly in a large piece of canvas carefully stitched together from remnants. The men would sit on the canvas and, they hoped, be protected somewhat from waves and sharks by the upper set of inner tubes. Paquito threw in

two ragged bedsheets as cover against the sun, four paddles, several gallons of water tied together with string, and
a dozen sandwiches wrapped in waxed paper.

"Let's go before Fidel changes his mind," Tommy
shouted.

"Or the Americans stop us from coming," Beto
answered.

"The currents will take us right to Florida," Paquito
said, smiling.

The four men firmly gripped their raft, two on each
side, and walked to the shore. Behind him, Raimundo's
lame leg drew a path to the sea.

During Adela's last year in La Habana, her dressmaking
business collapsed. Most of her clients had fled to Miami.
The ones who remained, telling everyone Fidel wouldn't
last, cursed their bad luck because they could no longer get
silks and satins for gowns. Some tore off their curtains for
Adela to make them new clothes, but they couldn't pay, so
Adela ultimately turned them away.

She did the next best thing she knew: she cooked. In
the evenings, she chopped and boiled bitter oranges and
lemons and stirred in the sugar a relative smuggled from
the refinery where he toiled during the week. She bottled
the preserves and sold them to the neighbors on her block,
keeping an eye out for members of the patrol committee
who denounced those failing to adhere to communist doc-
trine. After bribing the chairman, she sought customers
out on the streets, always encouraging buyers to return the
bottles by offering a rebate.

Excited cries from her sewing companions snapped her out of the past. The two women crowded around the television set.

"Más balseros," one yelled. "We can see them clearly, maybe it's my sister."

"Ay, mi tía, mi tía, please let it be her," shouted the other.

Adela pushed herself closer, peering into the small screen. There, in the waves, she saw him. She lunged for the volume control, but the steel brackets gave way and the TV came crashing to the floor, yanking the plug from the wall. The screen went blank.

Raimundo balanced himself on the sharp rocks littered everywhere on the dirty sand. He flinched as the cool water washed over his feet, laced into ripped-up, too large sneakers. Paquito, Tommy, and Beto took control of the raft, fighting for space on the shore with hundreds of others who shouted, ran, fell, struggled up, and ran again. The three men waded out a few feet and lowered the vessel into the water. Raimundo looked out over the landscape behind him.

"Are you coming?" Paquito asked.

"Claro."

The current pushed Raimundo forward, and, taking small steps, he reached the raft and helped to push it along. He hoisted himself onto it, settled his lean frame into an almost comfortable position, and grabbed a paddle made from a beach shovel attached to a short pole. His cousin and nephews did the same. With a coordinated effort, they dipped their paddles into the sea and pulled.

Soon the raft floated out at sea; the island of failed dreams stood solid in the short distance the group had traveled. Why had he waited so long? He remembered the days of revolution when he had rejected the values of his conservative family and joined the guerrillas. He hated Batista's treatment of the poor, his secret police, his arrogant speeches. What made Raimundo, rich and landed, sympathize with the poor? Fidel offered an alternative that he believed in, and for a while he felt useful, like never before. The poverty of the island, he thought back then, would be temporary before it would thrive as a more just society in the Caribbean Sea.

His parents were dead now, having breathed their last in their collapsing mansion now occupied by three families. They had refused to leave the island because of the art collection and antique furniture they wanted to save. His lover, a spirited seamstress he had never forgotten, had abandoned the island almost at the start. Years later, his wife and children followed suit. Now, here in the middle of the Straits of Florida, with the sun aiming hot spears at his face and arms, Raimundo breathed in, pulled on the paddle, and kept up a steady pace.

Thirty-six hours later, he drank the last of the water from his jug and shared the last piece of bread left over from a sandwich with Paquito. The two younger men, weakened by dehydration, slept with their heads on the inner tubes. His cousin, still alert, caught his eye and pointed. There, alongside their raft, the gray fin of a shark sliced the waves. Raimundo reached over and pulled the sleeping men closer to the center, tucking in their dangling arms and legs. He turned his back on the shark. The waves gained strength and smashed a wall of water over their heads.

Adela and her two companions lifted the TV set onto one of the sewing tables. "Is it broken?" Adela exclaimed. One of the young women plugged it into the outlet beside the sewing machine. "It still works!" she cried. The newscaster announced: "Four Cuban rafters have made the journey through the turbulent waters of the Straits of Florida to reach freedom just off the coast of Miami Beach." He added that the men were being taken to Jackson Memorial Hospital.

The story cut to earlier footage of the rescue group Hermanos al Rescate flying above four men sprawled on a raft. The news camera carried by an adjoining helicopter zoomed in as two of them slowly eased themselves into water up to their necks and pulled the raft toward shore with their last bit of strength. Dry foot! A third man lay prostrate on the raft, a mangled hand spurting blood, while the fourth tore a strip from his T-shirt and wrapped it around the wound.

The camera focused closely on the man on his back, eyes closed. Unmistakable. Decades-old memories threatened to stop her breathing. His once black chest hair was now white and dripping in tangled masses on his bare sunburned skin. A white beard covered sunken cheeks.

"I love you, and I'm not going to let you go." She heard his voice when she told him she was leaving the island. It had then been three years since Raimundo—part of Castro's victorious forces—had marched into La Habana that first week of January in 1959. Adela had thought her lover would come back dead from the struggle. Instead he walked into the city energized with a list of reformist measures Fidel had announced on Radio Rebelde from his hideout in the Sierra Maestra.

She tried to reason with him. "There's no future here," she insisted. "People are getting shot! They're just another repressive gang of thieves."

"Give it more time," Raimundo whispered to her, as he always did after a morning of lovemaking.

In 1965, time, for Adela, had run out. While he was at the office, she hopped on a bus and made a slow four-hour journey to Camarioca—the port opened by Fidel to malcontents wanting to leave—and slipped away on the first official boatlift out of Cuba, one that barely made the news.

Now, as if in a dream, she watched her former lover on TV, his arms sunburned, blistered, but still with the bulge of muscles that had once held her close. A scar—she didn't remember it—tore across the right side of his face to trail down deep into his collarbone. His T-shirt dangled off his shoulders, cutoffs threadbare. His bloody hand reached out, trembling. The helicopter moved on.

Adela walked back to her sewing machine. She rested her head on her hand, dazed, breathing hard.

"When will my family make it here?" one of her coworkers moaned. She flipped to the telenovela, the soap opera, on Spanish-language station Channel 51.

Shaking her head, Adela roused herself and pulled together the red strips and the white. She picked up the blue field of white stars. The same three colors as the

Cuban flag. She removed the strips, inseparable now, from the machine and placed them next to another attached pair on her table, clamping them under the presser foot, toes poised above the pedal. The thoughts jostling in her head sprung loose. He is in Miami. He made it. Only one in four survive.

At the end of the workday, five p.m., Adela pushed back the chair and stared at the wall shelves filled with rolls of red and white and blue fabric. She folded up the canvas strips and stacked a pile of blue rectangles neatly beside her sewing machine for tomorrow. She wrapped the back support around her waist, ushered out her two companions, and locked the factory door behind them.

Outside the building, her coworkers took off at a fast clip for home. Adela looked south: a former gas station now turned into a store for gaudy car tags, a low-income housing project, a Colombian restaurant. She frowned and turned her steps north on Seventh Street all the way to Jackson Memorial Hospital. The rapid comings and goings of patients, doctors, nurses, cars, and bicycles made her dizzy. She walked to the main entrance and up to the front desk. A flash of white light blocked her vision for a moment. She willed herself to speak.

"Is there a Raimundo Rivas here?" she asked the receptionist in Spanish.

"Yes, he has been moved from the ICU to room 334."

Adela walked out of the elevator and onto a polished granite floor. A blast of air-conditioned breeze tickled her bare arms. The sun pounded on the glass wall, which offered a view of the street. She marveled that Raimundo was safe at last, in the United States, which he had resisted for so long. The United States, whose freedom never quite made up for her longing for homeland.

What did she expect to gain? A return to the past? He might not even remember her. Why not turn around and go home? She walked back to the elevator and pressed the Down button, but then changed her mind and took a few steps toward the nurses' station. She stood still. What if he could not forgive her departure? She would say hello, if he was conscious, and leave.

Adela walked slowly to room 334, massaging her back as she went. She looked in past the half-open door. She pushed it wider. There he was, stretched out on the bed with an IV in his left arm, his face turned toward the window. Was he sleeping? Next to him, another man moaned in his sleep, head bandaged. She stepped into the room.

"Raimundo."

He turned his head. His eyes met hers with no sign of recognition, no flicker of emotion. Could it have been a minute? Five minutes? His pupils opened from the light at her back. Something else spread into his gaze. He extended his right arm in her direction and held up his bandaged hand.

"¿Eres tu, Adela?"

"Sí, it's me."

"Al fin."

Adela, at the bedside, reached up and trailed her fingers on the emaciated, sunburnt face. Raimundo lifted his other arm, tugging at the IV, and his hand gripped hers. He pulled her forward. She moved into the embrace she had imagined.

Rocking Chair Love

My wife is dead. Her rocking chair quivers slightly in the September breeze that floats here from a miles-away ocean swirling with the threat of a tropical storm. The woven cane seat sags, empty. She used to sit there, night after night. I watch the tips of the rockers scrape the iron grille of the narrow third-floor balcony of my Little Havana apartment. The sound irritates me; I can't crush the loneliness.

From the balcony, I look up and down Southwest Seventh Street and see my neighbors gathering on their balconies. Some call out to others in adjoining buildings, short squat expressionless edifices constructed just before World War II, when not a word of Spanish could be heard in Miami. My neighbors wait, as my wife did, for the sinking of the sun in the west, where the suburbs splay their fingers all the way to Homestead. They turn their eyes south and east, sighing and wishing they could see the lights of their left-behind city of La Habana.

I never bought into that pipe dream; better to live in the present. I'm retired, live on Social Security and what I make as a freelance public defender. I don't waste my time thinking about unfulfilled dreams or broken promises.

I sit in the other rocking chair and watch the cars speed past. Hortencia never understood why I didn't get up every day with fervor to save the world, as I had so many times claimed I would do. Truth is, coming down here from New Jersey, I couldn't break into the Miami lawyers' clique, and I just didn't try anymore. Hortencia had a good job, and I didn't need to work. Arrgh. The loneliness is too much to bear.

"Oye, Gastón, how's everything?" a man yells from the street below.

"My knee is messed up," I shout down.

"When are you going to Domino Park?"

"Maybe later."

"See you then."

Gastón knows he won't be going. An idea is forming slowly in his head, spreading out like butter over bread. Maybe it can work. The years of lawyering taught him that anything is possible. He leans forward and pushes himself out of the rocking chair. Facing the bathroom mirror, he shaves, slaps on Guerlain 1200 cologne, a favorite in Little Havana drugstores, and pulls on a starched light blue guayabera, a shirt with creases in the front just like the ones that colonial Spaniards brought with them for elegant gatherings in Cuba. Now everyone wears them, even women, trying to hold on to Cuban roots.

He doesn't look bad at seventy. No, indeed. No more overweight than anyone else his age. He wears his sparse hair slicked back with gel and puts his clothes to wash every day. He always smells clean. An article he read quoted life expectancy statistics. He could live another twenty years, and he doesn't want to live alone. What man does? Only women live alone. Men? Never.

Gripping the banister, he makes his way down the stairs, one step at a time, pausing every so often to let the arthritic knee rest from the pressure of his weight. The wind is dying down. He walks to Southwest Twelfth Avenue. At the corner he turns left and starts the fifteen-block trek to Jackson Memorial Hospital. The walk isn't unpleasant, but now Little Havana teems with newly arrived Cubans and Central and South Americans running from poverty and death squads, obsessed by the American Dream. He has nothing in common with them.

"Skills and education," he mutters. "They have none."

He makes his way past clusters of clattering buses and hives of workers coming home from construction sites. The evening is fresh, still with that hint of coming rain, but clear. He may not be walking alone the next time.

I have a lot to offer a woman. I'm a great cook. I love the nightlife, dancing tight to boleros and drinking a rum and Coke now and then. I'm not boring. I have a brain. Sharp, too. I'm just lazy. Here I am, finally, at the emergency room entrance of the hospital. How did I have the courage? Dios mío, I'm sweating. Even at night it's this hot. My guayabera is soaked. I think I'll sit in the breeze for a while to dry. I need to keep my eyes open to see who goes in and out. If anyone looks like he's dying, and if the only relative is a lonely woman, I must be ready to make my move. I hope Hortencia doesn't take it personally. She'll understand, like she always did about those things. Here comes an ambulance. Let's see who's inside.

Gastón moves closer to the entrance. The vehicle's back door slams open, and paramedics push out a stretcher holding a moaning man. They race inside. No one remembers the woman left behind. Dazed and unsteady on her feet, she climbs out of the ambulance and leans against it. She runs her fingers through her hair and smooths down her clothes. She holds on tightly to a battered Louis Vuitton shoulder bag.

Uhhm. She must be about fifty-five, a little plump from too many fine dinners out on Giralda Avenue, no doubt, but not bad looking. Dyed blond hair. I can see the roots. Droopy cow eyes. Dry. Shining red nails, some chipped. Brown slacks, beige blouse, wrinkled but elegant. She's probably someone who slathers on face cream at night, plucks her eyebrows, shaves her legs. Doesn't work. Materialistic. Somewhat docile. It appears she's alone.

Gastón walks a few paces to the hospital window and watches the paramedics roll the man into a room in the back. He looks at the woman who now stands at the entrance, reluctant to enter.

Maybe I can offer to take her to the desk and inquire about her husband? He must be her husband. Who else could it be?

"May I help you?" Gaston asks softly, feigning insecurity. Lawyers, after all, are actors. He's had to be inventive in his career, especially when dealing with his clients, crack addicts, drug pushers, petty thieves, prostitutes.

She turns her eyes, lids tattooed with black liner, to

meet his; then she looks him up and down in one swift movement. "Yes. Please help me."

"Is he your husband?"

"Yes. He's been very sick, but he refused to see a doctor. And now . . . this!" She shakes her fingers at the hospital window, angry, frustrated.

Gaston holds her gaze. He straightens his shirt and offers his arm. "Let's go inside, to the desk," he says. "I'll ask about his condition."

"He's the only person I have in the world. If he's dead, what will I do?"

"He'll be all right. What's his name?"

"Raúl Riverón."

At the reception desk, nurses shout orders to assistants. In a hallway, doctors pump the chest of an unresponsive man. On the floor, a young girl clutches a bleeding hand. A woman tears her dress off and howls, covering her head with the shreds of the torn garment. An intake worker kicks shut an open file drawer.

"We are here to inquire about Raúl Riverón," he says to the receptionist. "They just took him in."

"In surgery. Wait in the lobby."

Gastón leads the woman to a small lobby off the main floor. He slips some coins into a snack machine and selects a bottle of water. The woman sits down and sniffles into her hands.

"I shouldn't have yelled at him, but I was so tired of his insults," she said. "He turned gray and tried to speak. Then he slid to the floor."

"He will be OK. You'll see." Gaston pulls out his Guerlain-soaked handkerchief and passes it to her, along with the water. The woman reaches out, blows her nose, and sips from the bottle.

"He's dead. I know he's dead."

"They have miracle procedures these days. He will survive. What's your name?"

"Valentina."

"Gastón. I'm a lawyer."

Valentina nods and rests her head on the Louis Vuitton bag on her lap.

I'm going to stay here with her all night. She really smells good. What a perfume! She says she has no relatives, but if someone shows up, I'll leave. Or maybe I won't leave. I'll tell them I can help with any legal stuff.

Gastón leans back in the chair next to Valentina. They doze on and off through the night. Close to dawn, a disheveled doctor approaches Valentina, takes her hand in his, and shakes his head. She does not get up, just throws her head back against the wall and stares straight ahead. Her hand slips from the doctor's.

"I'm a friend of the family," Gastón says. "I'm here to help Mrs. Riverón make all the arrangements."

The doctor waves helplessly toward the desk.

Valentina and Gastón walk over. Holding a stack of papers the nurse hands him, he asks Valentina the questions, carefully prints the answers on the forms, and gives them to her to sign. He strokes her hands, her arms. She clings to him for one moment and drags her eyes to his. Reddened, bloodshot.

Beautiful eyes. I think I'm falling in love.

"I don't want to go home," Valentina says. "I can't face making the funeral arrangements. Let his sons do everything for once. He's their father."

"Does he have a will?"

"Yes. He left everything to me. But they don't know that."

She puts her hand on mine and looks at me, maybe wondering if her money is stoking my passion. Slowly I propel her out the door and west to Twelfth Avenue. The sun spurts its relentless dawn light on the sidewalk, rain clouds gone. The breeze carries in the smell of rotting sewage from the Miami River. Valentina doesn't notice any of it. She walks alongside me, fifteen blocks to my apartment on Southwest Seventh Street.

That night, on the balcony, we sit in the rocking chairs, and I ask her to marry me. She says yes.

Dime-Store Dare

It happened on a boring afternoon after class at Citrus Grove Junior High with nothing to do as usual. No one I knew stayed at school for extracurricular activities or went home directly to do homework. Our parents were newly arrived Cuban immigrants too busy crying for their lost island and working two jobs in Little Havana to care about what we did after school, so Gloria and Ibis and I boarded a city bus to downtown Miami looking for action.

In those days, malls didn't exist; downtown offered the best hangouts. We loved the pizza parlors, Chinese takeout counters, the library, Burdines, the Seybold Building filled with jewelry merchants, rows and rows of fabric stores packed to the ceiling with bolts of linen, satin, and silk, spending hours wandering around.

The bus pulled up in front of McCrory's, a five-and-dime where my mother—who was off today—worked as a cashier, and the only place we could afford. The store sat on the main drag, Flagler Street, where the homeless pushed shopping carts to Bayfront Park to camp underneath trees and sleep on park benches. Afro-haired teenagers from Overtown, the adjoining black community even poorer than Little Havana, begged for change. The Cuban boys, tired of being picked on by both blacks and whites, wore T-shirts claiming gang membership, Utes, Falcons, Double X, and challenged all on the street with stare-downs.

We sidestepped those sleeping on the streets, said no to the beggars, shoved aside the Cuban boys, and swaggered into the store. Laughing, joking, we strolled up and down the aisles, fingering strands of fake pearls and holding up flimsy polyester dresses to the mirror, imagining how the new garments would look on us. We opened the tops of perfume bottles, sniffed the scents, and spilled some drops on ourselves. We tried on eye shadow from a display.

At the hair products aisle, the rows of shampoos and conditioners grabbed my attention. Obsessed with pumping up my dull brown hair into voluminous locks, I bought hair treatments every time I had extra money. But no matter how many products I applied, no matter how much beer I mixed in with the Dippity Doo gel I used to set my hair on Campbell soup cans, my tresses remained flat and limp, unlike the stereotypical lustrous "Hispanic" hair I wanted.

"I bet you won't put one of those bottles in your purse and walk out with it," Ibis whispered.

"Mari, don't you dare," Gloria cautioned.

"Bet you I will." I slipped two L'Oréal oil treatments for damaged hair into my shoulder bag and said, "OK, let's go to Burdines."

We moved toward the exit, and just before we stepped

onto the sidewalk, a man wearing a gray shirt and pants flashed his badge at us. He was exactly my height, old and balding with tufts of white hair sprouting from his ears. His hands trembled.

"Follow me," he said sternly.

Ibis and Gloria burst into wails. I didn't move, looking him straight in the eye. "Who do you think you are, stopping us?" I demanded.

"Young lady," he said, "you're lucky you're under sixteen, because if not I'd put you in jail."

"I don't care," I shouted. "You are nobody!" I stood my ground and, brimming with the power of the young, felt confident that we would get out of the mess in no time.

"Come with me. The elevator is to the right." He placed his hand on my arm, and I shook it off, my face close to his. I could easily outrun him, I thought. Should I? I smiled, deciding I'd have more fun if I stayed, an adventure with no consequences. I craved this confrontation to prove to myself that I was in control of my haphazard life.

"Hijo de puta, don't touch me."

"Please, Mari," Gloria begged. "Don't say anything."

"Let's just do as he says," Ibis whispered.

Shrugging, I led the way, and we marched in front of the detective back into the store and into a small elevator hidden behind a tall rack of clothes. It smelled moldy, and I, who hadn't stopped cursing under my breath, got a whiff of urine as the elevator crawled up to the second floor.

"It stinks in here," I said.

The detective pointed ahead of him as the elevator doors screeched open. We walked into a drab room with peeling paint and pockmarked floors where two security guards sat at a table doing newspaper crossword puzzles.

"Call their mothers," the detective said, looking relieved that he was leaving. "They were shoplifting."

"Adios, cabrón," I called after him.

The security guards snickered and continued their puzzles, ignoring us as we sat without speaking on hard chairs. Finishing his task, one of the guards pushed the newspaper aside and asked each of us how to reach our parents.

"Carajo, are you crazy?" Ibis's mother shouted as she strode into the room. She grabbed her daughter by the arm and shoved her out the door while Ibis wept, begging forgiveness. Gloria's parents arrived next. "¡Ayyy, Dios mío! Help my daughter," her mother screamed. Her father narrowed his eyes at me. Gloria hung her head and sniffled. Neither one of my friends pointed to me as the culprit, nor did I volunteer the information.

While I waited for my mother, I spent the time entertaining the guards.

"Can you sing *Cecilia Valdés*?" I asked. They shook their heads. I filled my lungs with air and, in a shaky falsetto, let loose the famous line from the famous Spanish operetta: "¡Yo soy Cecilia Valdés!" They laughed. I rattled off a conversation in French I had learned in class: "Où est la bibliothèque? Est-ce là-bas?" We were good friends by the time my mother arrived, hours later, from a babysitting job she had on her days off.

"Mari," she whispered, knocking timidly on the door and stepping into the security office.

"Don't worry," I said. "Everything is OK."

I waved to the guards, who waved back.

At home, my mother called my father, who lived with his new wife some miles away.

"Don't tell anyone else about this," he warned when he had me on the phone.

As for me, I had known all along I wouldn't be punished, one parent too busy with his new life, another too depressed to think straight. My afternoon of crime confirmed that I could get away with anything, and I quickly forgot it.

Here in Havana

Dishes slipped from her hand, the car wouldn't start, the air conditioner stopped cooling. She waited in vain for calls and visits from her children, but they lived their lives as if she didn't exist. Fifty years of the deadness of exile, the struggle of immigrant life, the anonymity of refugee status had drained Iraida's will. The longing for a lost Cuba, kept alive through old photographs of her early life there, forced her to stay in bed for days at a time.

I can change my life, she said one morning, examining wrinkles in the mirror.

Iraida gave notice at the hedge fund, withdrew cash from her accounts, packed the books from her seven bookcases in sturdy boxes—Dostoyevsky, Plato, Didion, Balzac, Nin, Hemingway, Woolf, too many to list—and shipped them to a warehouse in Havana. She sold her condo on Biscayne Bay, purchased a visa at the airport, and boarded a plane to her lost island.

I'm going back home, she said.

From the plane window in the early dawn hours, the island of Cuba appeared as a sprawling green-and-brown alligator floating on a burning sapphire sea. Iraida gripped the arm rest and pressed her face to the glass. Most of her fellow passengers saw nothing magnificent in their arrival, having made this journey many times to bring relatives the things most coveted in this land of have-nots: American dollars, phones, clothes. Some of the others were Americans from religious organizations. Or Australians and Canadians on vacation. No one was there because of haunting memories that drove a search for peace.

In customs, she examined the officials, the first Cuban "communists" she had ever seen. She wanted to ask, "Why did you choose the other side?" And, "How is your life?" She couldn't tell whether her observations were clouded by decades of anti-Castro, anticommunist discourse on Cuban American radio, TV, street corners, cafes, and she tried to weigh both sides equally, but all she ended up doing was wishing the questions inside her head would stop.

Outside, a giant poster asked all "compañeros" to work for the common good. She hailed a cab, and they drove past buildings with peeling paint, crumbling walls, past people in shabby clothes or designer jeans from America, over never-ending potholes, as 1950s cars and Chinese bicycles whizzed by. The old world had vanished, but she could see remnants of it in the colonial buildings, la Catedral de la Virgen María, Paseo del Prado, el Parque Central, el Hotel Nacional, and they helped match memories with reality.

"What's wrong with the Cuban soul?" I once asked an Argentine friend.

"Cubans can never really go home," he answered.

The driver turned into the Cementerio de Colón on Calle 12 in the Vedado neighborhood. She knew where her grandparents were buried from a note her mother had written long ago. She touched the tombstones.

These are the only relatives I have on this island, she said.

Their stories, and her parents' stories, from the fifties, forties, thirties, so vivid in her mind she felt she had lived them. Sometimes she didn't know whether she really remembered an event, a place, a relative, or the memory came from pictures, kept in boxes, and pored over continually, an obsession with a past that floated just out of her reach, evading ownership.

"Take me to a hotel," she told the driver.

He drove her to Casa Habana in a neighborhood within walking distance of the Malecón. The ground floor, locked up and littered with chipped tables and rickety chairs, sparked her imagination. She rented it at once from the owner, who looked closely at her hair, her nails, her shoes, imagining what riches she had accumulated in the United States. In a few hours, a delivery truck dumped her book boxes inside.

Offering cash, she convinced two young men standing at a street corner to build display shelving out of old wood they located at a demolition site. They arranged the bookcases against the walls in the front, setting up the abandoned chairs and tables in a circle. An adjacent kitchen held an old espresso coffee maker, an old refrigerator, and a stove. In the back, next to a bathroom, she made up the small space into a bedroom with a mattress she bought from a black-market vendor.

The next day she registered with the US embassy and went to a government office to pay for a business license. All around, private establishments—with government encouragement—advertised their products and services. Cubans operated their own restaurants and repair shops, bakeries and beauty parlors in their homes. They turned their cars into taxis and rented spare bedrooms.

My business will thrive here, she said, and my heart will heal.

Wearing her new uniform of shorts and T-shirts, she strolled to a market and stood in line to get supplies from nearly empty shelves. She paid in cash for overly ripe mangos, bananas, mamey, loaves of Cuban bread, dented tins of espresso coffee, and two cardboard boxes to make signs. Her neighbors used ration cards to get their groceries.

I hate communism, she said, it destroyed my life. But I'm here to reclaim what I lost. I don't care about blackouts, water shortages, or rationing.

Back home, she tore the cardboard boxes apart and, with a marker, lettered signs on each piece. One said Libros. Others announced: café, 25c; café con leche, 50c; tostadas 25c; batidos 50c. She placed the signs around the front windows and on the front door and unlocked it, adding another sign: Abierto. She sat at a table, chose a book by Jean Rhys, and read: "Reading makes immigrants of us all. It takes us away from home, but more important, it finds homes for us everywhere." After a week of waiting, the people came.

Visitors from Canada, Spain, Latin America, Germany filed in, along with curious locals, browsing through her books, ordering café con leche and sitting in chairs and on big cushions she had bought and scattered on the floor. When she ran out of coffee or milk, she turned to the black-market vendor. On a wall, she contrived a message board for visitors to advertise their services and products. She organized evening poetry readings in Spanish and English. She hired neighbors to play guitar and drums and sing.

I will die here, she said, though I may have to marry to stay.

Soon Alberto came knocking. In the past she would have turned him away, a bald fiftysomething with two missing teeth, but she didn't, opening her door and her heart at the same time. As she sold books, Alberto, in the kitchen, percolated coffee and blended smoothies.

At a discussion group she had started, the locals shared their stories. She listened silently. They talked about Robertico, the twenty-year-old incarcerated for possession of Ritalin, a popular drug for Cuban club revelers, his girlfriend going by bus to Combinado del Este to see him each Sunday.

"I'm in love with him," she said.

They marveled about someone's niece Marita, the abandoned mixed-race girl who lived in a state orphanage set up in the opulent mansion of an American fugitive rapper.

"None in her family can afford to take her in," a neighbor said. "She now lives in luxury."

They spoke about Josefa, a fourteen-year-old whose

parents shoved her into a makeshift cage when she lost her mind, running naked through the streets, stabbing walls and bushes with a kitchen knife.

"We didn't want her away from us," said her mother, "even if hospitals cost nothing."

They laughed about the lovebirds Patricia and Manuel, posada travelers, paying four dollars a night for a room in one of hundreds of dirty houses scattered around the island for a few hours of sexual passion, with cockroaches crawling the walls, and sheets that were rarely changed.

These stories were part of her new native land. She heard no stories of the 1950s when the island boasted the largest middle and professional class in Latin America and where every American product could be found. All of that had been wiped from memory here, but none of the tales could match the one she left untold. Out on the Malecón one early evening, sitting on the seawall and dangling her feet above the water, she remembered.

Iraida saw sixteen-year-old Iraidita, living with her sister in a rundown hotel on Miami Beach, waiting for Fidel to fall so they could go back home. The teenager shivered in the cool ocean breeze the night after the hurricane when, racing her collie Joaquín on the grassy mounds of Lummus Park, she heard a scream.

She turned toward the moonlit sea, hair falling in strands down her back, wet from the rain, open mouth like a cave. More cries, and she recognized the voice of her twelve-year-old neighbor. Sprinting to the shore, the collie at her side, she saw Marusa III sink into the churning waves, struggle to come up for air, and disappear. Iraidita dove in. Alongside her El Médico, another neighbor from the hotel, fought the current, both of them reaching Marusa III at the same time.

The two dragged her up onto the sand, the doctor pumping the limp girl's chest and blowing hard into her mouth. "Call an ambulance," he had yelled. His daughter, running up, paced in circles, tearing at her hair. Marusa III's mother writhed on the sand. Marusa's grandmother, on her knees, called out to the Cuban-African spirits Obatala and Yemaya. The doctor stopped pumping and stared up at the moon.

"She's left us," he said.

Iraida got up from the concrete ledge and contemplated the Straits of Florida. She thought she saw the flickering lights of Key West. Marusa III, fifty years ago, had gazed in the opposite direction and believed that lights from Cuba winked at her. Two shores separated by a void of sea brimming with remembering and forgetting, death and grief straddling the heart. Marusa III, like Iraida, could not resist the temptation to get back home.

I'm here, Marusa, she said, for both of us.

The wind whipping her hair, her T-shirt, she stared up at white clouds forming a hallway leading into the endless purple haze of the heavens. There, against the remarkable sky above her native island, she saw Marusa III, maybe smiling, black hair, sapphire-blue eyes, her disabled hand held tightly to her heart in the pose of a praying mantis, maybe nodding, suspended inside the cloud corridor.

The past is too strong, she said.

Iraida looked away from the images in the sky and dug

into her jean pocket, retrieving two now crumpled flowers, a white and a blue. With a flip of the wrist, she cast them into the water.

For you, Yemaya, goddess of the sea, she said.

She turned her back on the killer ocean and walked on, the cement of the Malecón rough against her flip-flops. She reviewed the bookstore's calendar in her mind: a reading tomorrow, an art exhibit the day after, a writing workshop on the weekend. She marveled at the family of friends she had made and the warmth she felt in her new home.

She wondered if Alberto could concoct daily lunch specials for their customers. She entered the store and, in the kitchen, mixed banana smoothies and set them on the table.

"On the house," she called out.

Acknowledgments

Eternal gratitude to my beautiful and beloved mother who, while suffering debilitating illness, jump-started my writing life when she enrolled me in a fifth-grade creative writing class.

Heartfelt thanks to everyone at the University Press of Kentucky, particularly to Lisa Williams, New Poetry and Prose series editor, who offered brilliant insights, and to Ann Marlowe, the sharp-eyed copy editor.

Many of these stories were written while I attended Florida International University's MFA Creative Writing program, with advice from caring professors. Thank you to my mentor and thesis consultant Dan Wakefield, acclaimed author and screenwriter, for helping me find the courage I needed to write. Dan gave this book its title. Thank you to Lynne Barrett, in whose class I learned the necessity of plot, and to department chair Les Standiford for booming out, "Is it on the page?" My time as a student with this trio of professional writers enriched me beyond words.

I am indebted to the Cuban community that has never ceased to inspire me, many within it telling me their stories of suffering and bouncing back.

Much gratitude to three special friends for their support: television producer Isabel Bahamonde, who brainstormed with me during the difficult writing stages, photographer Juan Siller for shooting the video for my book trailer, and playwright Ross Levine for editing the script.

To my wonderful sons and daughter, Christopher, Andrew, and Alexandra—always at the forefront of my life—thank you for offering so many new perspectives. I love you.

THE UNIVERSITY PRESS OF KENTUCKY
NEW POETRY AND PROSE SERIES

This series features books of contemporary poetry and fiction that exhibit a profound attention to language, strong imagination, formal inventiveness, and awareness of one's literary roots.

SERIES EDITOR: Lisa Williams

ADVISORY BOARD: Camille Dungy, Rebecca Morgan Frank, Silas House, Davis McCombs, and Roger Reeves

Sponsored by Centre College

 CENTRE
COLLEGE